I0687179

Henry: To Prove Himself Worthy

Henry: To Prove Himself Worthy

Mansfield Park Continuation, Episode 1

LEENIE BROWN

LEENIE B BOOKS
HALIFAX

Contents

Dedication

To Patty,
who sparked the idea for this book when she wished to
know
if I could write a piece that made Henry Crawford
redeemable
I hope I have succeeded.

Dear Reader

At the end of *Mansfield Park*, Jane Austen wrote:

> *Let other pens dwell on guilt and misery. I quit such odious subjects as soon as I can, impatient to restore everybody not greatly in fault themselves to tolerable comfort and to have done with all the rest.*

It is my goal in writing the books found in the *Other Pens Collection* to take up my pen and continue the stories of various Austen characters who were at fault in some way in Miss Austen's novels. In these stories of redemption and reformation, I do not look to dwell on the characters' guilt and misery so much as help them find a way to overcome their failing and find their own happiness.

This collection is and will be an ever growing and shifting creation until such time as the stories seem to have all been written. How the final arrangement and allotment of stories will look, I cannot say. However, as of the publication of this book, *Henry: To Prove Himself Worthy*, I can tell you that *Through Every Storm* will be placed in this collection as the first *Pride and Prejudice Other Pens* book, and Henry's story will be only the first in a series of tales featuring characters from *Mansfield Park* as well as some completely original characters whose lives have in one way or another been intertwined with Henry's. As these stories are written, you will be given glimpses of how Henry's life unfolds after he finds his happiness at the end of this tale.

Chapter 1

Henry Crawford paced the edges of the ballroom, surveying the latest crop of debutantes with a critical, assessing eye. Not just any beauty would do for him this season. The lady he selected to pursue would need more than beauty to capture his admiration. He had had his fill of games, dalliances, and chits who thought too well of themselves. He was looking for a woman of substance who would stand by his side as his wife. Not that he truly felt worthy of such a lady.

His eyes narrowed as he scrutinized a group of ladies standing in a corner to the right of the ballroom door. There were several in the group who stood head and shoulders above the rest. They would never do for him. He did not possess great height, and a gentleman must not have a partner — even for a dance — who was taller than he.

Of the ladies of acceptable height, there were those who held their chins very much like a particular young lady whom he would like to forget. She was full of airs and invitation, but... He shook his head. Maria Bertram had been more beauty than substance, and what substance she had possessed was, as it turned out, unpleasant. He shuddered in remembrance of that particular lady's sour disposition. Then there were one or two in the group who were of a proper stature and appeared shy — almost fearful. They were the ones whispering to their chaperones and fidgeting uneasily. They would likely be the ones still standing by the wall when the dancing began — not because they lacked beauty, for they did not. Some were slightly more attractive than others as was the normal scheme of things, but all were elegantly dressed and expertly coiffured, showing themselves to best advantage. However, their reserved manner and lack of sparkle would likely see them overlooked. That might be the best place to begin, with the wallflowers, if he could bring himself to approach anyone at all.

He paused at the door to the terrace, which was not quite closed, and pulled in a gulp of cool air. The room seemed rather warmer than he remembered it being. Perhaps it was the crush of people, or — he swallowed at the strange uneasiness that rose in his throat — perhaps it was the disapproving eyes of the many matrons and male folk guarding their precious treasures that made him wish to pull at his cravat and straighten his jacket and caused him to feel so warm. That was likely it, he had to admit to himself. He had always been welcomed in the past, but tonight he did not feel that former welcome. It was his own doing, however, and he knew it. Had he considered one sweet lady as the precious treasure she was, he would likely not be here scouting for someone with fair eyes and a pleasant smile to fill the void that Fanny Price had left in his heart.

"Have you settled on the next scandal?" Charles Edwards drew up beside Henry and lifting his quizzing glass, looked down his nose as he surveyed the room. "It is an excellent crop with many beauties."

"Aye, it is that," Henry agreed with a half smile.

"Which shall it be?" Edwards cast a quick glance at his friend of many years.

"I do not know. I see their beauty, but..." He turned toward Edwards so that his lips could not be read by anyone.

"I do not think I am ready for this," he admitted in a low whisper. "I should not have allowed you and Linton to talk me into attending."

"Do not be foolish, my man, you are exactly where you must be to assuage a disappointment." Edwards' smile had a wolfish quality to it as it usually did when he was speaking of ladies. "A broken heart does a lady good. It hurries her on to consider matrimony at a faster pace. In reality, their guardians should be thankful for those of us who provide such a service."

Henry chuckled. If there was one thing at which Edwards was good, besides seducing a lady, it was twisting logic into some rational explanation about why his actions were not so reprehensible as most might consider them. The truth was that Edwards was a rogue through and through, but he had enough charm and good looks to make him not only acceptable to many young ladies but also desirable. Likely one of them fancied herself as capable of ensnaring the man's heart and reforming him into all that was proper. Henry wished her well, for the task would not be an easy one.

"The Price chit you liked. She's married now, is she not?" Edwards pressed his point.

For a moment, Henry paused to consider that Edwards might be correct. After Henry's departure last spring, Fanny had not been long in securing an offer from her cousin Edmund. He shook his head. No, his friend was not correct, for Fanny's heart had not been broken, and that was a truth which, as of yet, never ceased to cause his own heart to pinch. She had been kind to him and caring, and perhaps she might have been persuaded to love him, but she had not loved him as he had wished she would.

He knew his foolishness had hurt her, and he imagined her disappointment in him had been great. How could it not have been? Fanny was all that was good. She scowled — very prettily and softly — at all that was less than virtuous. How she must have censured him in her heart, if not in her words! And he deserved it. He knew he did. He had failed her. He had acted rashly, in a fit of misguided passion. He was likely very unfit for any lady of such good taste and character.

Henry's morose contemplations were brought to a halt as a burly gentleman wearing a green jacket attempted to pass between Henry and the doors behind him. "You must dance at least once before you escape." Trefor Linton gave Henry a nudge with his shoulder. "When the horse tosses you on your arse, you have to ride it again."

Henry flashed a grin at his friend. "You are not also going to tell me how breaking the hearts of poor innocents is somehow a service to them, are you?"

"Good heavens, I should say not!" cried Linton. "Has Edwards been spouting his regular rubbish?"

"I will have you know it is not rubbish," Edwards defended. "Why just last year, three young ladies made very eligible matches after I had shown them particular attention. I tell you, I am a good luck charm for the matrimonially-minded miss."

"I dare say at least one of them felt a very pressing need to accept the first offer she was given after receiving your attentions." Linton raised his left brow and looked down his nose imperiously at Edwards.

Edwards shrugged. "I heard no word of scandal."

"That is because you refuse to listen," Linton muttered.

Henry shook his head. How Linton had remained friends with Edwards and him for all these years was a mystery. Linton was level-headed and honorable to a fault.

He would never be caught in a dark corner with a chit. Edwards, on the other hand, made it something of a sport to see how many dark corners he could frequent with a different chit in each one. And Henry? Well, he was more inclined to participate with Edwards and tease Linton for his refusal to join them than he was to deny himself such pleasure. He drew a breath. No longer. He hoped.

"So who shall it be?" Edwards prodded again. "Her?" He directed his gaze at a curvaceous blonde to their left. "She would be quite delightful, I imagine."

Linton's long arm reached behind Henry and thwacked Edwards. "Have a care. That's Hodson's sister."

"Indeed?" Edwards did not remove his eyes from the lady. "I had not thought such beauty could be found in his family." He tipped his head as he studied the beauty across the room. "She has definitely defied the Hodson odds and lost her awkwardness. Does Hodson still frequent Gentleman Jackson's?"

Linton nodded. "Daily."

Edwards lowered his glass and gave it a wipe before putting it in his pocket. "Then who else might there be of interest?"

"Start with Constance," Linton suggested. "No harm will befall you. She will be all that is proper, and perhaps others, seeing that I trust you with her, will stop scowling at us. It is very unnerving. How do you bear such looks of displeasure so frequently, Edwards?"

Edwards laughed. "The pleasure of a few stolen moments is worth the discomfort, my friend. You should try it."

"Not likely," Linton retorted.

"You know Crawford is nearly as skilled as I at finding secluded corners." Edwards once again had his quizzing glass out and was wiping it. "I am surprised you would trust your sister with him."

"It is one dance in my presence, and he knows I would kill him if he were to so much as think of stealing a kiss from Connie." Linton crossed his arms and glowered at Edwards. "I believe Crawford currently has enough sense to heed such a warning, and that is why I will allow him to dance with my sister. You, however, still lack such sense and are to keep your distance."

Edwards shrugged. "Her tongue is too sharp for my liking." He answered Linton's growl at the disparagement with a smile. "I prefer not to be lectured when I am attempting to seduce a lady."

"I should give such ungentlemanly comments the reply they deserve, but knowing they will likely fall on deaf ears, I shall spare my breath. Come, Crawford," said Linton. "We will leave Edwards to his dissipated ways and go find Connie."

~*~*~

Constance Linton huffed softly as she stood beside her aunt.

"Stand up straight and do not scowl." Gwladys Kendrick's instructions to her niece were accompanied by an appropriately stern look and a slight nudge forward. "No man will ever find you if you attempt to sink into the shadows."

"I would be quite happy not to be found." Constance favoured her aunt with a charming smile.

"Do not be ridiculous, child. There must certainly be at least one gentleman here that will rise to your exacting standards of dullness," a smirk pulled at the corners of Aunt Gwladys's mouth.

"Dull is not the proper word, Aunt."

"Yes, I know. Intelligent, forward thinking, and so on." Aunt Gwladys waved her hand in a small circle, indicating that she knew Constance's description of her ideal gentleman would go on and on for some time if she was allowed to begin such a topic of conversation. "Many intelligent beasts, such as your brother, dance, you know."

Constance linked her arm with the lady who had been her companion and guide for these past six years, filling neatly the void left by the death of Constance's mother. "I know. I just find this whole sifting through the dross process to be quite tedious."

Aunt Gwladys patted Constance's hand. "Ah, but the prize for such effort is well worth it." Her brows furrowed, and her lips pursed for a moment as she caught sight of her nephew. "Why your brother insists on keeping some of his friends, I will never understand."

"Because one does not turn out a stray just because it has a bad eye — or some such thing," replied Constance with a laugh.

"There is more than an eye that is bad with that one," Aunt Gwladys muttered as her nephew and Henry Crawford approached.

"He is not so bad as Mr. Edwards," Constance whispered. "In fact, Mr. Crawford has been making improvements, according to Trefor."

She was not certain why she felt compelled to defend Henry Crawford. She did not hold him in high esteem herself, but there had been an aura of melancholy about him lately that was so unlike him. She had never been one to enjoy seeing the suffering of others even if they did deserve to feel wretched. Of course, she knew that it would likely not keep her from reprimanding him if the opportunity arose. It was a serious inconsistency in her character, and one she wished to remedy. But, should she continue to reprove and learn to bear the sorrow of the transgressor without qualm, or was it better to bite her tongue and pat the offender's arm while saying "there, there, poor dear"?

"Mr. Crawford," Aunt Gwladys gave a nod of her head in greeting while her features spoke of her hesitance in doing so.

"Mrs. Kendrick, Miss Linton." Henry bowed and smiled. "It is a pleasure to see you. You are both looking fetching tonight — quite the brightest jewels at the ball." He took the hand that Aunt Gwladys had offered him and gave it a kiss.

"Your silver tongue will not work with me, young man. I know your sort." Her tone was stern despite the small smile that played at her mouth in response to his flattery. "And your lifted brows and raised chin will not scold me into being civil," she said to Linton while tapping her cheek with her fan, indicating that he should kiss it.

Linton obliged. "Tonight shall be trying enough for Crawford. There is no need of increasing his discomfort," he said softly.

"Consequences are consequences," Aunt Gwladys retorted.

"You are correct, of course, but they are not for you to award or laud," her nephew responded.

Henry pulled at his sleeves and attempted to keep a smile on his lips. How many times had he had to plaster such a look of nonchalance on his face over the last year? "Linton will not allow me to leave until I have danced," he explained.

"You were leaving just after you arrived?" Constance asked in surprise.

Henry shrugged. "I might have found the card room for a while before making my exit, but yes. I am uncertain I am prepared for the close, and may I say just, examination, I appear to be receiving."

"Surely, you knew it would be thus?" Constance snapped her mouth shut and smiled sheepishly at her brother, who had cleared his throat rather loudly at her comment.

"I expected as much," said Henry. "However, I had hoped some of my infamy had faded."

"There are likely many gentlemen in the card room whose only interest in your past activities is to place a bet on if they are likely to be repeated," said Aunt Gwladys. "The ladies tend to be longer in coming to terms with the idea of accepting a gentleman back into society who has shown disdain for the solemnity of marriage. They fear you will be unfaithful as a husband, you see. However, you are not without your particular charms." Her lips curled into a smile. "Pin money and an estate with ample carriages and servants as well as a townhouse and fine gowns are very alluring to some young ladies."

"Crawford is a changed man, are you not?" Linton turned to Henry. "Henry here has learned the value of a good woman, and that is precisely what he seeks — not some fortune hunter." Linton waved his hand as if brushing away some disgusting bit of dirt.

"I am trying to be," Henry replied as the musicians began to play something recognizable rather than just the few notes of tuning they had been playing for some minutes.

"I have assured Crawford that you would be happy to partner him for the first dance if Aunt Gwladys has not harpooned someone else for you."

Constance's mouth dropped open at the audacity of such a statement. "I can assure you that I would have garnered several names on my card had I wished to do so. I do not need them to be harpooned."

Henry bit back a smile at the way Linton's sister crossed her arms and glared at her brother. He had seen them nearly come to blows before over some careless comment that Linton had made and to which Constance had taken exception. It did not matter that she was half the size of her larger and older brother. While others might find the man intimidating, his sister did not. There was no denying the fiery blood of the Kendrick family ran in the lady's veins. In fact, she seemed to have received all of her own on that account as well as a portion of her more relaxed brother's.

"She would have secured many a partner, had she not been doing a valiant job of avoiding the majority of them," muttered her aunt.

"Then, am I in luck?" asked Henry with a bright smile for Constance. "Might I have the pleasure of enduring the stares of the masses with such a lovely partner to hold my attention?"

Though she knew him to be a charmer, Constance had to admit, as she accepted his offer and his arm, that Mr. Crawford's words were very pretty and did make a lady feel a particular happiness that crept unbidden to her cheeks.

Chapter 2

"You dance very well," Constance said when she and Henry had completed their set.

Henry inclined his head in acceptance of her compliment. "And your performance added credibly to mine. We were well-matched. Did you enjoy yourself?" He knew that she had only accepted his offer to dance because her brother had decreed it would happen. "You did not feel too put upon, did you?"

Constance blinked in surprise. "No, I was not put upon in the least, and though I do not particularly enjoy balls, I enjoyed that set of dances. You are a lively conversationalist even when there is little time to converse." They had spoken of rather mundane things — the weather, the decor, her aunt's rose garden — nothing of importance, and yet, it had not been dull. Henry's expressions had added some interest, as had his occasional witty remark. Constance had felt herself in very good company.

"You mentioned your stables," she said as they

approached her aunt and brother. "I had not realized you had been at Everingham. You did not call."

Henry had nearly always called on her brother when he was at his estate and Trefor was at Linthurst. Henry even called occasionally when Trefor was not at Linthurst just to see that all was well with her and Aunt Gwladys. She had always suspected that Henry did so with the hoped there would be a need for him to turn around and ride back to town with some message for Trefor instead of proceeding to Everingham.

"Crawford has spent a good amount of time on his estate — sorting it out and seeing to improvements," Linton said. "I called on him."

"He came to lend a hand," Henry explained. "I know my way around an estate to some degree, but your brother insisted I needed further instruction."

"And he did." Linton gave a sharp nod of his head to punctuate his point.

"I can tell by your expression, Miss Linton, that I have surprised you."

Constance's mouth had dropped open the slightest amount, her eyes had grown wide, and she had blinked several times. It would have been a most charming expression if Henry did not know that his doing what was merely the common duty of an estate owner had been the cause of it.

"I thought you disliked the country." Her cheeks reddened at not having been able to better regulate her expression.

Henry's replying smile was tight. "It is not that I dislike the country, but rather that I have always found it and the responsibility that accompanies it dull.'

Constance gasped, and before she could think better of it, she replied, "Responsibility may not always be pleasant, but one should not simply avoid it because it is dull." Constance did not know which was worst — the way her brother cleared his throat and scowled at her, the displeased hiss from her aunt, or the shadow of sadness that passed across Henry's face.

"Proper ladies do not lecture," her aunt whispered. "Not even if the gentleman deserves the reprimand." She raised a brow in Henry's direction. "You do not wish to be labelled a shrew, my dear."

"She was not lecturing," said Henry.

The small, sad smile that accompanied Henry's gracious words — that, Constance decided, that was the worst response to her unguarded comments.

"And," Henry continued, "she is correct. One should not neglect responsibility in favour of pleasure. I have learned that it can be very costly, and that is a lesson I do not wish to repeat." He bowed. "I have danced my one dance and will now take my leave. Thank you, Miss Linton, for providing me with a most enjoyable reintroduction to society." He turned to leave but paused and turned back. "Might I call on you tomorrow?" He looked from her to her brother. He did not know why he wished to call on her exactly, but for some reason, he felt a strong desire to spend time in the presence of a lady who, knowing his sins and censuring him for them, did not spurn him but treated him with respect.

Linton shrugged. "Do you wish it, Connie?"

"She would be delighted," said Aunt Gwladys before Constance could do more than open her mouth. "We are always pleased to have you call at Lindhurst. The fact that we are in town should not change that."

Henry thanked Mrs. Kendrick but sent a questioning look toward her niece.

Constance nodded. "We would be delighted," she assured him.

"Until tomorrow then." Henry made one more bow and took his leave.

"I am surprised that after all your disapproving remarks you would wish to have him call on us," Constance whispered to her Aunt.

"One does not cast out a stray because he has a blind eye." Aunt Gwladys winked at her niece. "Besides, I believe he has indeed changed," said Aunt Gwladys as she watched Henry make is way past several young ladies, who were doing their best to attract his notice. "Did he flirt with you, Connie?"

"No, he was pleasant and charming, but he did not flirt. Of course, that is likely because I am his friend's sister."

Aunt Gwladys rolled her eyes. "And no man has ever married the sister of a friend."

"Aunt Gwladys, you cannot be meaning to match-make!"

"No, no, no," her aunt assured her. "As I have told you several times this week, I will wait until your third season before I begin to arrange matches — and it will not be with the likes of Mr. Crawford, whether he has changed or not — well, at least not until I am assured that this reformation is lasting." She shook her head and huffed slightly as if it were quite taxing to have to explain all of this. "I was just attempting to make a point, although I am not entirely certain what it was now."

"I believe your point was that Crawford did not flirt with Constance because he knows I would thrash him if he did so; therefore, he is perhaps a changed man," supplied Linton.

Aunt Gwladys scowled. "You threatened him?"

"Every time we have met since Constance turned sixteen."

"Well, that does take a bit of the sheen off my point," grumbled Aunt Gwladys.

"Only a bit," Linton assured her. "It was still a valid point. He is changed — or changing, as it may be."

Aunt Gwladys sighed. "Stand forward, girl. No gentlemen are going to see you if you stand in your brother's shadow." She turned a hard look on her nephew. "You have not threatened every gentleman of your acquaintance, have you?"

Linton shrugged. "Only the ones I felt needed it."

"Oh, good heavens," cried his aunt, "I think I will withdraw my promise. I shall have to devise a match for you, Connie."

"No," said Constance. "You will not go back on your word. I have this season to find a match of my choosing."

"Then stand forward, and, Trefor, go fetch me a glass of something to drink or go find a partner for a dance or go play cards — it does not matter what you do so long as you do not do it here where your presence will frighten away your sister's prospects."

Linton laughed, gave his aunt's cheek a kiss, and wandered off toward the card room.

~*~*~

Henry had made it almost to the door of the ballroom when a familiar voice calling his name stopped him.

"Henry! Is that you?" Mary Crawford hurried toward her brother.

He stopped and, taking the hand she extended, placed a kiss on it.

"You have not called," she scolded before he could say so much as a word. "You did not even write to our sister with your intention to return to town. She had thought, and I agreed most heartily, that you might defer your return to society until a few weeks into the season." She gave him a knowing smile. "I knew you could not stay away forever, however. You are too fond of pretty things and company."

She wrapped her arm around his and stepped closer. "Rushworth was recently wed. November, I believe it was, so you are safe on that account. He will be much too busy and happy to bother with you." She stepped away slightly. "She is a beauty and much more pleasant than the previous Mrs. Rushworth. Is she not, Flora?"

"Lady Stornaway," Henry greeted the lady that had come to stand next to his sister with a dip of his head.

"Indeed, she is much more pleasant and better acquainted with the need to be discreet if one wishes to retain her position within society." The feather in Lady Stornaway's cap fluttered as she tipped her head to survey Henry. "You are looking well. It appears this little incident," she made a small circular gesture with her hand, "has not had an ill effect on you. I have several friends who are desirous that I invite you to a dinner as soon as you returned to town — and it was not just your sister," she assured with a quick flick of her brows. "I will send a note around. You are at your townhouse, are you not?"

"At present, I am." He wished he was not. He wished he had an address that neither his sister nor her friends knew. Many of his sister's friends were very much like the women his uncle, the admiral, kept as friends and lovers — ladies, who had secured a comfortable position in the upper layers of society but had failed to do so in such a fashion as to be entirely pleased with their position. "I am afraid I will have to disappoint you, however. I am not in town for a lark."

Mary laughed and swatted his arm playfully. "Don't be foolish, Henry," she chided. "You are always looking for an adventure. Life is dull without them. Is that not what you have always said?"

"I believe I have had my fill of adventure," Henry replied.

"Your fill of adventure! Let it not be so!" Mary cried. "I have become the sister of an insipid brother, Flora. How greatly you should pity me!"

Lady Stornaway gasped and looked appropriately affected before Mary continued.

"You cannot still be regretting Fanny," Mary said with some force. "She is but a silly girl, whom I shall never forgive, and not only for not having accepted you. For if she had, we should both be happily married."

"Yes, well, that has not happened." Henry covered her hand that still lay on his arm and lifted it off. He would extricate himself from this conversation much more easily if he were free of his sister's grasp. He would also be free of this discourse if he were to be direct with his sister. She was too practiced at twisting his words when he was anything but forthright. "However, marriage is my purpose in coming to town, and since Lady Stornaway's friends are neither single nor of the stripe who place great importance on the vows taken before a parson, it would be best if we kept our meetings to soirees such as this."

Mary gasped while Lady Stornaway looked affronted.

"Let me put a point on it for you, my dear sister. Had I not attended that last party at your persuasion and had I gone to Norfolk as I had planned, we might both be happily married. But," he dropped her hand and held up a finger to mark his point, "you wished for me to see Mrs. Rushworth. You thought there would be great entertainment in it. Do not cast this debacle at Fanny's feet. She was the only one in this whole sorry tale who was without guile. She refused me because she knew I was not worthy of her, and I was not — as anyone who reads a paper or sits in a drawing room with a cup of tea knows, I was not. And with that blackness attached to my name, I shall have a difficult enough go of it trying to find a lady of substance to accept me. To throw myself back into the society I kept before..." He shrugged and shook his head. "It would be foolish. Therefore, I will gladly welcome you and your friends at soirees such as this, but I will not be accepting any invitations to private parties, save for those held by Dr. and Mrs. Grant. I will call on them next week after I am truly settled in town." He bowed to the gaping women and hastened out into the corridor.

"That was some speech," Linton said from his place of repose against a column, causing Henry to stop his progress to the door and freedom from the stifling confines of society. "Lady Stornaway will not be pleased."

"Nor will my sister," Henry replied.

Linton tipped his head toward the door. "My aunt sent me away. She thought my presence was scaring away all of Connie's prospects."

Henry chuckled as he and Linton exited the building. "You do cut an imposing figure."

"I try to," Linton replied with an easy smile. "It keeps the blackguards away. I wish to see Connie well settled."

Henry nodded. "I wish I could say the same for my sister."

"You do not wish to see her in a good situation?" Linton asked in surprise. He motioned down the street and began to walk.

"Oh, I wish her to be happy. I just fear it shall never be." Henry shrugged. "You have done much better for your sister than I have for mine."

"I had parents to do most of it," Linton replied. "You had the admiral, but he was not a good example, and his wife was too indulgent."

It was not the first time Henry had heard Linton's opinion on this matter, and he could not fault his friend for his words, for they were true. Mrs. Crawford had doted on his sister, teaching her all there was to know about shifting in the best society and snaring a man of means. The admiral had likewise taken Henry on as a protégé of sorts. The admiral was a charming and clever man with an easy smile for a pretty woman, no matter her age or marital status. His own marriage seemed to mean little to him beyond having a beautiful hostess to preside over his parties. If the admiral saw something, or rather, someone, he wanted, he would scheme his way into her bed. Lies were only punishable when they were spoken to him, but never when they were used in claiming what he desired. All this, he had impressed upon Henry. Henry would be a man of means, and as such, he should enjoy his status. It had been a pleasant idea to a young man who dreaded giving up his carefree existence. If only he had been willing to give up that unfettered lifestyle when his sister required it.

"I should have taken her to Everingham instead of Mansfield. I should have taken her there even before that." Henry had rehearsed over and over to himself the events that had led him to Mansfield and into the presence of the Bertrams and Fanny Price. He knew precisely the points where disaster could have and should have been avoided. He also knew he could not go back and undo what was done, but in contemplating his errors, he hoped not to repeat them.

"Yes, you should have, but you did not."

Henry sighed. Linton was that sort of person who did not try to smooth over the deficiencies of his friends just to lift their spirits. He never went out of his way to find times to point out their errors, but if the subject of some folly was broached, he would not gloss over it. To Linton, it was best to recognize the error for what it was and learn from it. Trying to soften the fault, or to deny it, was foolishness of the greatest kind, and Henry had come to agree with him in recent days.

"I fear it is too late to be of any good to her," Henry admitted.

He and Linton walked on in silence for some distance down the line of carriages before Linton spoke again. "Your sister will likely do what she wishes, but there is a chance that your example might impress something upon her. You have just this evening made a lasting impression, I dare say."

"She will likely deem me a fool. She will have to if she wishes to keep Lady Stornaway as her friend."

Linton shrugged as he stopped and turned back. "It is likely, but in her heart, she will ponder what you have said. She is fond of you, you know."

Henry nodded slowly. "I know, and despite how it might have sounded tonight, I am also fond of her. However, I cannot allow my love for her to sway me from my purpose."

"No," Linton agreed. "That you cannot do."

"She persuaded me away from what I knew I should do to secure an excellent wife once. I will not allow it again."

Henry clasped his hands behind his back and watched his foot flick a pebble off the walkway. "It is possible, is it not, for me to become a man deserving of an excellent wife? Am I capable of becoming what my uncle was not?"

Linton clapped him on the shoulder. "Aye, I think it quite likely."

Chapter 3

Henry pulled at his sleeves as he stood behind the butler at Linton's, waiting to be announced. Feeling an unpleasant flutter of nerves at calling on a lady in her home was not something Henry had experienced before, especially when that lady was the sister of his friend. In fact, he had called on Constance and Mrs. Kendrick many times without the slightest twinge of anxiety in the past. However, today was different, and he suspected it was due at least in part to the decisions he had made last evening after he had departed the ball.

"Mr. Crawford to see Miss Linton."

Henry gave his sleeve one more tug as Mr. Atkins stepped to the side and allowed him entrance to the sitting room. Henry greeted Mrs. Kendrick and the lady seated to her right first and then took a seat near where Constance was finishing a conversation with Miss Barrett, the daughter of the lady seated next to Mrs. Kendrick and a particular friend of Constance's. He squirmed slightly under the scrutiny of Miss Barrett's mother as he sat, waiting.

"Evelyn, we must be going." Mrs. Barrett stood, and her daughter followed suit. "It was a pleasure," she said to Mrs. Kendrick. "But we will not overstay our time and keep you from your other caller." She gave Henry a sweeping look. Her lips curled in displeasure.

The action made Henry bristle. "I am not contagious," he muttered.

The lady's expression changed from assessing to one of shock.

"You looked as if I might cause some ill to befall your daughter," Henry explained, settling back into his chair and crossing one foot over the other. The lady expected him to be a cad, so he might as well conduct himself with the nonchalance of one. "I assure you I will not. Miss Barrett is lovely, but not the sort of lady to tempt me away from my single life." He smiled. "And that is what I seek — a wife. And, might I add, since it is likely that it will be discussed in my absence, I do not intend to be the sort of gentleman to take a wife lightly or my vows to her as anything less than sacred."

"Is that so?" Mrs. Barrett asked in surprise.

"Shocking, is it not?" Henry replied.

"Indeed, it is," said Mrs. Kendrick with a stern look at Henry.

Henry inclined his head in acceptance of her reproach. "I have erred quite remarkably on that account," he admitted.

"You most certainly have," Mrs. Kendrick agreed. "But it might be best not to lead with such declarations when calling on young ladies."

"I only wish Mrs. Barrett and her daughter to know I mean them no harm, so that when we meet again, they can feel at ease." It was part of the plan he had formulated last night as he sat before the hearth with only a bottle of wine to keep him company. He would not shy away from acknowledging his errors. It had been uncomfortable to be direct with Mary, but had he continued to thrust and parry with her and Lady Stornaway, he would have likely found himself unable to refuse an invitation to some gathering and would, therefore, find himself in precisely the position he wished to avoid.

"I shall keep that in mind," Mrs. Barrett replied. "You will not fault me, however, for being skeptical of your words."

Henry brushed at a wrinkle on his sleeve. "I should fault you if you did not."

"Then we have an understanding," said Mrs. Barrett. "And if you should require a partner for a country dance and will promise to walk no further with Evelyn than the dance floor, I will allow you to dance with her."

It was Henry's turned to be startled.

"Mr. Linton and Mrs. Kendrick have, I assume, given you leave to call on Constance, and I trust their judgment more than I trust your words." She pulled on her gloves as she added. "I have been a friend of Mrs. Kendrick for many years, Mr. Crawford, and I appreciate directness. However, I will keep watch at soirees and in the paper."

Henry smiled and nodded. "If there is any indiscretion on my part — beyond what I have already committed — I shall not approach your daughter."

Mrs. Barrett tapped her nose and then extended a hand to her daughter. "We do have other calls, dear."

Evelyn dutifully took her mother's hand, and they took their leave.

Constance stared at Henry as her friend departed. This was not the Henry she knew. She knew a gentleman who was charming to a fault, who was always saying or doing whatever might be most pleasing to any lady in the room. He was the sort of gentleman who avoided declaring any of his own actions as overly bad. They might be ill-thought-out or a small folly, but they were never an error of a remarkable size. She had always enjoyed Henry's company, but she had never found him the least bit compelling — annoying, prevaricating, and amiable despite his faults — he had been all of those things, but never compelling — until now.

"I have come to a conclusion," Henry began in an attempt to lay out his true intentions for calling on the ladies at Linton House today.

"That you shall offend everyone you meet who looks at

you with a wary eye?" Mrs. Kendrick's eyes danced with amusement.

"No, well, perhaps," Henry's fingers drummed a pattern on the arm of the chair in which he sat. "I suppose it might come to that. But my intention is to avoid hiding my folly. I dare say it is a well-known story from the looks I received last night and from Mrs. Barrett just now. What point is there in denying my part in the seduction? I was led astray but not unwillingly."

"Must you speak so directly?"

"I apologize, Miss Linton," Henry smiled at the lovely blush on Constance's cheeks. His former self would have considered how he could make those cheeks so beguilingly flushed again and again; however, his present self only paused for a moment to admire her beauty before continuing. "I did not come to discuss the particulars of what has happened in the recent past, although they are the foundation for my request of you."

"Your request?" Constance repeated his words, her brows drawn together and her lips slightly pursed.

Again, Henry took a moment to admire her before replying. She was remarkably charming.

"Yes, I seem to be at a loss on how to proceed in society as a respectable fellow. I know very well how to be a cad and libertine, but I have pitifully little idea how to be the sort of gent that a lady of good character and strong morals would wish to take on as a husband. Therefore, I would greatly appreciate your assistance." He held her bewildered gaze for a moment before looking to Mrs. Kendrick. "I know no other lady of exemplary character who might be allowed to help me." He paused and drew a deliberate breath to stop the small clenching he felt in his chest.

There was one lady of exemplary character who, at one time, would have likely helped him learn all he needed to know to be worthy of her, but at that time, he had not been so willing to learn as he was now. It had, unfortunately, taken the crushing of his own heart at his own hands to make him willing to learn. Mary had always said that Fanny Price would be the making of him, and she would be, for it was the loss of her that saw him here, now, hoping with all that remained of his fragile heart to be given the assistance he needed.

Constance blinked and looked from Henry to her aunt and back, her hand rested on her heart which was beating a steady and somewhat rapid rhythm. "You think I can help you learn how to be a husband?"

Henry nodded. "You are a lady of good character, so you should know what someone such as yourself would wish for in a husband. You could point out my shortcomings, and we could devise a way for me to overcome them."

He leaned forward in his chair and turned his attention to Mrs. Kendrick. "Trefor has helped me learn much about running my estate, and he could likely aid me with this, too. However, I should think the information would be more reliable coming from a lady."

"You have no ulterior motives?" Mrs. Kendrick held Henry's gaze. "I do not need to fear for my charge's virtue or heart? You are a charming rascal, and she would not be the first to fall victim to your enchantment."

"I promise you," Henry begged, "I would never attempt anything with Miss Linton."

"Why not?" The words flew from Constance's mouth before she could think better of them.

"Constance!" her aunt chided. "Do you wish to be seduced and ruined?"

Constance wished to be swallowed by the settee on which she sat or to fall through the floor or to simply disappear. Speaking of seductions was not something she wished to do with anyone, especially not her aunt and Mr. Crawford! But she had allowed her words to run faster than her thoughts, so now she must explain them or face a lecture on the dangers of gentlemen like Henry Crawford.

"I did not mean I wished to be seduced." Constance kept her voice soft, and her eyes on her clasped hands in her lap. "I was merely wondering if there was some defect in me that would make me less worthy of a gentleman's consideration." There were defects. Plenty of them. She preferred reading to dancing. She liked to speak of things of importance rather than just the weather and who was wearing what and doing this or that. She liked to know and understand the working of an estate and its books. She was curious about how crops could be improved or flocks strengthened. Added to this, she was known to speak her mind too freely and contradict people. None of these traits recommended her as a desirable, biddable wife.

"There is no defect in you, Miss Linton," Henry said, placing a reassuring hand for a moment on Constance's until her aunt cleared her throat and gave him a stern look. "I would not have asked for your assistance if I had not thought you were perfection personified. It is true," he stressed to Mrs. Kendrick, who was looking at him skeptically. "I am not flattering her."

"Then why would you not consider me?" She had not thought her cheeks could get any warmer, but she was wrong, for they felt as if they were about to burst into flames as she realized how her question might sound. "I do not mean consider me for a seduction, but just consider me as someone you would court and marry — not that I wish for you to court or marry me." She clamped her mouth shut before she could explain her way into some other situation that would require even more explanation.

Henry couldn't help the way his mouth curled in pleasure at seeing her so flustered. "Your brother," he replied simply. "I will not deny that I find you attractive, but I would rather like to keep my life and all my body parts whole."

"Oh." She dared not look up at him. He found her

attractive? It was not that she thought herself unappealing, but she had not supposed a gentleman such as Henry would give a lady such as herself a second thought. "You do not find me too outspoken or bookish?"

Henry sighed. "Fanny was bookish," he said softly, causing Constance to look up at him.

There was a sadness in his eyes that caused her heart to ache for him. "You loved her?"

He nodded and then shrugged. "Not enough, I suppose."

"I should like to hear your thoughts on that," Mrs. Kendrick said. "As Trefor tells it, you had proposed marriage to this girl, and yet, you say you did not love her enough." She rose and went to the door. "The decanter of sherry," she said to Atkins.

"This call is going to require something stouter than tea," she said in explanation to Henry and Constance, "for I am considering allowing you to help this poor unfortunate soul, against my better judgment." She held up a hand to forestall any comments from either her niece or Henry. "I am not agreeing to help; I am merely considering."

She returned to her seat and looked at Henry expectantly. "I believe the explanation of your statement will sway me one way or the other, and if it is as I suspect, and you are perceptive enough to realize it, then my consideration shall become a tentative agreement."

Henry's brows furrowed. "I am not certain I understand your meaning."

Mrs. Kendrick waved the comment away. "It will become clear eventually. Proceed."

Henry rose and paced to the window. He knew that proposing such an idea as being told where his failings were would require some fortitude to listen to criticisms. He had not considered that he would be required to speak of Fanny. However, he seriously doubted that he could find another lady of Fanny's caliber to accept him if he did not secure some assistance. So, drawing a deep breath and releasing it in a rush of air, he began. "If I had loved Miss Price enough to prove my worthiness as a husband, I would have gone to Everingham to please her rather than staying in town to attend a party to please my sister."

"True," Mrs. Kendrick agreed.

"Miss Price and her happiness should have been my focus."

"And it was not?" Mrs. Kendrick asked.

Henry shook his head. "Obviously not."

Mrs. Kendrick motioned for the tray containing the decanter and glasses to be placed on the table next to her chair. "We will not be receiving any more callers today, Atkins," she said as she dismissed the butler. "You say obviously not, Mr. Crawford, but to delay a trip to please a sister seems a reasonable thing."

Henry blew out another breath. He had thought that very thing when the idea had been proposed to him by Mary. A short delay was not of any great significance, after all. He had gone over these things in his mind a dozen or more times, chiding himself for his foolishness, as he came to terms with having lost Fanny.

"I did not attend the party just to please Mary. I was curious. I wanted to see how Mrs. Rushworth was getting on with her husband." He shook his head. "He was an oaf compared to her, so I expected to find her miserable."

"That is rather uncharitable, is it not?" Mrs. Kendrick asked.

"Oh, indeed, it is, I suppose. But Mrs. Rushworth was so lively and quick, and Mr. Rushworth was so — not."

Mrs. Kendrick shrugged. "Unequal marriages are not so uncommon. One often chooses the most prudent choice. I assume Mrs. Rushworth accepted Mr. Rushworth for his wealth?"

Henry nodded slowly. "She knew it was her duty to marry well, but she would have refused him had another put forth an offer — even if his standing was slightly less."

Mrs. Kendrick's smile was knowing. "But you did not offer for her. Why?"

Henry shrugged. He had known Maria wanted him to make an offer. It was not as if she had been backward in her attentions nor had she dissembled about her prefer-ence for him over Rushworth. Her words, her looks, the small touches, and the passionate embraces in various hidden corners had spoken loudly of her desire for Henry. However, to him, she was a dalliance, a lady with whom to have a bit of fun. It was heady having a beauty such as Maria Bertram, who was promised to another, so much in his power. "I did not wish to marry."

"Why?" Constance covered her mouth with her hand. She had intended to sit quietly and just observe, but once again, her tongue had been faster than her better judgment.

"I will venture that Mr. Crawford was enjoying his status as a single young gentleman and did not wish to be parted from his carefree pursuit of pleasure."

Henry felt his face warm under Mrs. Kendrick's stern glare.

"But he proposed to Miss Price."

"That he did, my dear, but again, I will hazard a guess that Mr. Crawford's heart was not engaged in regards to Miss Bertram nearly so much as his desires were." Mrs. Kendrick poured a small glass of sherry for her niece. "However, with Miss Price, who was likely more circumspect and did not fan those flames of desire in the fashion that I suspect Miss Bertram did, there was time enough for Mr. Crawford's heart to begin its work on his mind. It was then that he began considering marriage."

Henry accepted the glass Mrs. Kendrick handed him. "That is true," he admitted. "It was simple enough to engage Miss Bertram's affections. Miss Price was more determined to not be affected by my charms." He took a sip of his drink. "I do not believe her capable of being swayed by the charms of any gentleman who was not her cousin." His lips turned downwards in a scowl.

Mrs. Kendrick's brow rose. "Do I hear jealousy?"

Henry shrugged. He had been — no — he *was* jealous of Edmund Bertram. "Why should I not be jealous? The man has all that I had hoped to attain." He turned toward the window. "Edmund had always had it though. Fanny's heart was not free to love another so long as her cousin remained single." He shook his head at himself. "It is also my fault that he was not happily wed to someone other than Fanny." He watched carriages pass on the road outside as the room fell into silence for a few moments.

How foolish he had been to suppose that a dalliance such as he desired when he sought to make the cold and off-putting Mrs. Rushworth once again the warm and welcoming Miss Bertram could be concealed and quickly forgotten after the moment of pleasure had passed. Pleasure! What a heinous word! Promising delight and delivering sorrow!

He turned back toward Mrs. Kendrick. "I sought only to please myself. I desired, so I pursued. I wished to be the smile on Mrs. Rushworth's lips instead of her husband." He huffed at his own shameless behaviour. "It was a game — one last game before I took up the mantle of responsibility I knew I should have worn all along." To his surprise, Mrs. Kendrick wore a smile when he finally lifted his eyes to her.

"As I thought. You are not lost entirely to your reprehensible ways." She drained the liquid from her glass. "And I think you are already in possession of the most important pieces of knowledge you need." She filled her glass again. "Ladies are not play things. Love and marriage are not trifling matters with which to sport." She lifted the decanter in an invitation to fill Henry's glass again, but he declined.

Henry nodded and sank into the chair he had first taken upon entering the room. It had been a lesson hard learned. The scars of it would likely not heal for some time. "Will you allow Miss Linton to help me to learn how to treat a lady properly? Please?"

Mrs. Kendrick's brows drew together and her lips pursed as she gave Henry a long assessing look, before draining her glass of sherry in one large draught. She shook her head and huffed as she looked toward the ceiling as if she was struggling to understand herself. "Yes," she said after she had lowered her eyes to his. "Do not make me regret this decision."

Chapter 4

"Crawford," Linton greeted the next afternoon as he entered the sitting room where Henry was waiting for Constance. "What brings you to my house again today?"

"Do try to sound civil," Aunt Gwladys chided from her corner. "Remember that Mr. Crawford is your friend."

Linton raised a brow at his aunt. "I remember precisely who Crawford is, and I see his curricle in front of my house and wish to know why."

"He is taking Constance for a drive at my request." Aunt Gwladys spared only a glance up at her nephew from her stitching. "Do you not remember that Constance and I are helping Mr. Crawford learn to be a proper gentleman?"

"You said you were going to instruct him on how to treat a lady."

"And we are."

"By sending Constance out in his curricle with him?"

Aunt Gwladys nodded and peered over her spectacles once again at Linton. "There is no better way to learn something than by doing. So, Mr. Crawford is going to practice courting a lady on your sister. There is nothing to fear. Constance is not so retiring that she will not tell him where he is going wrong, and you have been threatening the man with bodily harm for several years, have you not?"

Linton growled, and Henry worried the brim of his hat. "If you harm her or her reputation, I will see you pay."

"I know, you have said so several times, and I do not doubt your words," Henry replied. He swallowed as Linton stepped close enough to his side that their shoulders were touching.

"Do not break her heart," Linton whispered, "or I will pierce yours."

"I have no intention of engaging her heart."

Linton scowled. "See that you don't."

Constance stopped at the doorway. She knew that her brother had said he threatened Henry on a regular basis, but she had never seen it until now. Though she did not hear any exchange of words, she could tell that Henry was not just uneasy but fearful. To give him time to compose himself and to spare him any embarrassment, she stepped back from view and called out cheerfully that she was ready as she entered.

Henry smiled at her. She was lovely. The blue of her eyes was heightened by the blue of her pelisse and hat. "Shall we go then?"

Constance shook her head and grinned. "No. A gentleman should always compliment a lady on her looks before they depart. We like that sort of thing. Begin again." She caught how Henry darted a look at her brother. "He shall not harm you for saying his sister is lovely." She crossed her arms and glared at Trefor. "Unless, of course, he thinks she is not."

"Do not be ridiculous, Connie. You know I think you are beautiful." He crossed the room to give her cheek a kiss. "I just find it difficult to hear other gentlemen say it."

She patted the hand that had grasped hers. "Then do not listen." She chuckled at his huff. "Mr. Crawford and I are only friends. He requested my help, and I am providing it." She tipped her head and smiled up at her brother.

"Be careful," Linton cautioned.

"When am I not?" Constance asked.

"You do not wish for me to answer that. However, I will say that you are intelligent enough to know how easily plans can go awry."

"All will be well," Constance assured him. "Now, my pupil awaits to tell me how fetching I look." She gave his hand a reassuring squeeze. "You can question me about every detail over dinner."

She turned away from her brother and back to Henry. All would be well, she assured herself. She could entertain the attentions of a charming gentleman without falling under his spell. This was Henry Crawford, after all. She had never before fallen for his pretty words. Of course, that was before he had taken on his current persona. No, she shook herself mentally, this was Henry. All would be well.

"You look lovely," Henry said as he approached her and offered his arm. "Now, shall we go?"

She nodded and placed her hand on his arm. "That was much better. However, in the future, a more specific compliment might be better. You might wish to mention the colour of my ensemble as being flattering or some such thing."

"Not with your brother present," Henry muttered.

"Are your intentions less than honourable?" she questioned in a teasing voice.

"No."

"Then you should not fear what a brother or guardian might think. They do the same when they greet ladies. I have heard Trefor do it."

Henry laughed, looking over his shoulder at Linton. "Perhaps I should not fear your brother, but I do." He gave Linton a knowing nod and was rewarded with something less like a scowl and more like a smile as they left the sitting room.

~*~*~

Henry handed her up into his curricle before climbing up next to her. "You are certain you do not mind being seen in public with me?" He had surprised himself by worrying a great deal, as he tossed and turned on his bed last night, about how she would be viewed by the ton if it appeared he was courting her. He had not courted a lady for any noble purposes in the past. He had feigned honorable intentions, but he had only one thing in mind — capturing the affections of the young lady as far as she would allow him to capture them and her. He had never been serious in his pursuit of any lady, and that is what the ton knew. They did not know that he was a man on a mission to change his ways.

Constance smiled and shook her head while a nervous flutter took up residence in her belly. She had discussed with her aunt what the gossips might say, but her aunt had assured her that with a brother such as Trefor and Connie's own exemplary behavior, there would be little on which the wagging tongues would be able to build their stories, save, of course, for Henry's previous behaviour. However, Aunt Gwladys had insisted that his new behaviour and respectable ways would soon over shine all that.

"I had only wished for you to tell me my errors and help me figure out how to overcome them. I did not mean for you to become so actively involved in my education."

"It is one drive, and I am confident not many will take notice of me." Constance was not certain if she was attempting to reassure him or herself. "And it they do, they know my brother."

Henry nodded slowly. Trefor Linton was known for being upstanding. He never gambled to excess nor was he given to drinking or flirting. "I dare say they will notice me and, therefore, you," Henry cautioned. "It might be best if we just retired to the drawing room, and you wrote me a list of things to do and things to avoid."

She tipped her head and studied the set of his jaw. There was a muscle that was twitching. He seemed genuinely nervous about where they were and what they were doing.

"You are not afraid to be seen with me, are you?" she teased, causing him to cast a surprised glance her direction.

The twinkle in her eye and the way her lips puckered as she attempted to keep from smiling caused him to draw a quick breath as he reminded himself of whose sister Constance was. No matter how fetching she might look, he was not to indulge his appreciation of her.

"I am not afraid to be seen with you, but I am rather worried about your being seen with me. I am not the best catch of the season." He glanced her way again. She was smiling broadly.

"Not yet, but you will be," she said with a laugh. Then turning more serious, she asked quietly, "You are genuinely concerned about my reputation?"

"I am." He gave her a crooked smile. "And not just because your brother promised to run me through if I damaged it. You deserve to make a good match, and I should wish to run myself through if I were the cause of your not being able to make one."

"It is one drive," she assured him.

He shook his head. "And one musical, and one trip to the theater, and one ball, and one whatever other thing your aunt thinks I need to experience before I am deemed worthy to be on my way."

"All will be well. We shall weather the whispers together." She smoothed her skirts and turned her eyes toward the road. "I do enjoy your company."

"You are far too good." He saw a smile pull at the corner of her mouth, and he could imagine the sparkle that was likely in her sapphire blue eyes.

"Yes, I am, but then, that is why you chose me," she replied.

~*~*~

"How was your drive?" Linton asked his sister as they dined that evening. "Crawford behaved himself? There will be no lines of scandal in the paper?"

Constance raised a brow and took a sip of her watered down wine before she replied. For some unknown reason, it rankled to have her brother questioning her. She had been on drives with other gentlemen — not many, but two or three — and Trefor had not deigned to interrogate her after those outings beyond asking if she had a pleasant time.

"We had a delightful time. The weather was warm with only a few clouds to threaten our enjoyment." She took another sip of wine and returned her glass to the table before taking up her cutlery to begin eating the pheasant that had been placed before her. "The weather seemed to bring out one and all. There were so many people to see and greet."

Linton nodded his understanding. "It was a beautiful day for an outing," he admitted. "But what of Crawford?"

She knew her brother would not let a question go unanswered, no matter how many times she might attempt to dodge them. Yet, it annoyed her that in asking such a question, he was not only demonstrating a lack of trust for his friend but also for her — not that he was likely aware of the fact that he was doing so. "Do you mean to ask if I am the sort of lady to allow a gentleman to take advantage of me and ruin my reputation?" She attempted to keep her tone light and her smile sweet.

The bit of food Linton was about to eat hung on his fork in the air and then returned to his plate. "Of course, I am not questioning your behaviour. I know you to be very proper, but Crawford is not known for his propriety."

"Then, you do not trust him?" Constance asked nonchalantly.

"No." Her brother said around a mouthful of food.

"Did you not claim he is a changed man?"

"Yes, I believe he did," Aunt Gwladys replied.

Constance gave her aunt an appreciative smile and then turned her eyes back to her brother and waited for his response.

"I.... it's just..." he stammered as he swallowed his food. "I worry about you," he finally admitted. "I should hate to see anything unsavoury being said about you or for you to fall into something for which you are not prepared."

"Then it is true; you do not trust me."

Linton could hear the hurt in his sister's voice. "It is not that. I do not trust the rest of society. There are those who will sensationalize even the smallest indiscretion into something that is ruinous."

"Yet you allowed Mr. Crawford to dance with me in the view of many of those gossips." Constance crossed her arms and glared at her brother. "You saw no harm in helping your friend with his estate or in giving him a nudge to attend a function or even in asking him to dance with me. Explain yourself."

Linton huffed and then fell silent. For several minutes the only sounds in the room were the clinks of metal against china. Finally, when his plate was empty, he leaned back in his chair and began his explanation.

"Crawford has proven himself capable of change — I will give him that —, and he was a quick student when it came to estate matters —, but then he has always been more intelligent than one would assume. I also know his heart is desirous to amend his ways, but you must realize how precious you are to me, Connie, and there is the possibility that Crawford may stumble a time or two before he gets things right. Making an error in adding up sums in an account book is nothing compared to tarnishing or ruining the reputation of a lady such as yourself."

Constance could not fault Trefor for his concern. She had spent several minutes yesterday discussing something very similar to this with her aunt, and then she had contemplated it again as she went to bed as well as while she dressed for the day. There had been a small sense of unease that had rested in her stomach until Mr. Crawford had expressed his concern for her reputation.

"He was every inch a proper gentleman," Connie said with a reassuring smile for her brother. "We drove for a while before getting out for a bit of a stroll. He was all that he should have been, truly."

Her brother's shoulders relaxed as he expelled a breath.

"I was fearful at first that we might not even make it to the park," Constance added. "Mr. Crawford was hesitant."

"About what?" her aunt questioned.

"He feared what being seen with him might do to my reputation. He insisted it might be best if we return to the house, and I just give him a list of things to do and not do."

"He was concerned about —"

"My reputation," Constance nodded as she finished her brother's thought. "You have nothing to fear. I am perfectly safe with Mr. Crawford." Safe as far as her reputation went that is. Her heart, well, that might be a completely different story if Henry continued to be the sort of gentleman he had been on their drive. He had seen to her comfort in all situations. He had allowed her to speak on whatever topic she chose, and he had not once lifted a disapproving brow or cleared his throat uneasily when she had strayed to topics generally thought unusual for a lady to consider. He had even quoted poetry a time or two. He really was a most entertaining and amiable companion, and one she looked forward to seeing again and often.

Chapter 5

"Good evening, Mr. Crawford," Mrs. Barrett greeted as Henry approached the group where Constance was standing.

"Mrs. Barrett, ladies, Linton," he replied as he bowed. "I apologize for my tardiness. The carriage line was longer than I expected it to be." He had actually gotten out of his carriage and walked the length of a dozen carriages in an attempt to be on time, yet, a quick look at his watch when he arrived told him that he was a full ten minutes late. "I shall begin my journey much earlier next time." This last bit was said quietly to Constance.

"You truly were not attempting to avoid the event?" Constance kept her eyes roaming the crowd as she tapped her fan on her hand.

Mr. Crawford did not have the looks of an Adonis, but in that particular shade of green, he was rather handsome. However, to openly admire him would be a faux pas of no small proportion. For one thing, her aunt and brother would once again commence their interrogation of her opinion of Henry as they had after yesterday's walk and the trip to the theatre the day before that and the visit to the museum three days ago. For another thing, it might give Mr. Crawford the mistaken notion that she wished for him to be more than her pupil — which she did not — not really. Did she? Oh, he did set her well-ordered thinking on its end.

"No," Henry replied, wishing that she would look at him instead of everyone else in the room. She had been avoiding making eye contact with him for two days now, and though she took his arm when he offered it, her touch had become lighter than it had been on their first few outings. She had also been more circumspect than normal in standing or sitting an appropriate distance from him.

"I am looking forward to the performances." He smiled as she turned a questioning look on him. "Most of them. I am certain there will be a few that we shall have to suffer through."

"Shall we take our places then?" Aunt Gwladys asked. "Mr. Marsh has looked our direction several times in the past five minutes."

"He has shown particular interest in Evelyn," Mrs. Barrett whispered behind her fan.

"I had noticed," Aunt Gwladys replied with a smile. "There are seats near him."

"Marsh is a toad," Linton grumbled. "Always croaking

on about the most boring things and clearing his throat." He shook his head in disgust.

"We were not attempting to match you with him," said Aunt Gwladys. "And that toad has a very good income. Now, hush and lead us over there."

Henry barely kept back a chuckle at the way Linton's eyes narrowed and he let out a soft growl of displeasure.

"I shall not accept him if he comes asking after Connie," he told his aunt as he offered her his arm and dutifully led the party over to be seated near Mr. Marsh.

As they neared their destination, they were intercepted by Mr. Edwards. "Linton," he said, "you must come sit with me, or I shall be bored to tears."

"Why are you here?" Henry asked. He suspected he knew the reason for Edwards' attendance, but that reason and his asking Linton to sit with him did not match.

"To see and be seen," Edwards said as he fiddled with his quizzing glass. "Although so far, I have not seen what I had hoped."

"We were going to see if Marsh would allow us to sit with him," Linton said.

"That toad?" Edwards asked in surprise. "Surely, ladies of such beauty as your sister and Miss Barrett could do better than a balding gentleman fifteen years their senior."

"It is not ours to decide who is or who is not an acceptable choice," Henry said quietly. "That is up to the ladies and their guardians." He kept his eyes fixed on Edwards, whose brows had flown to his hairline.

"That is quite right," agreed Mrs. Barrett.

"And the ladies chose to sit with a toad?" Edwards asked.

"He is not a toad," Miss Barrett replied. "He is a gentleman. A kind, considerate gentleman."

Edwards sketched a bow. "My apologies. It appears I have spoken out of turn." He gave one more bow and took a quizzical look at Henry before moving on.

Constance watched him go and then turned to Henry. "That was well done, but does he truly need someone to sit with him?"

Henry shook his head. "No, he will find someone to join him either in his seat or a secluded corner."

"Likely both," Aunt Gwladys murmured.

Henry inclined his head in acceptance of the truth of her statement. He and Edwards had attended several musicales together over the years. They were ideal places for certain activities if one could convince a lady to slip away from the crowd during a performance.

"Do you believe that?" Constance asked as she took her seat next to him.

"That Edwards will find a willing lady? Yes," he replied. "He is proficient..."

Linton cleared his throat and glared at Henry, who shrugged.

"I was only answering a question. I did not broach the subject."

"Proper gentlemen do not speak to ladies of ... conquests," Linton whispered to Henry before turning displeased eyes on his sister. "And proper ladies do not ask about such."

Constance's mouth dropped open, and her eyes flashed. "As if I would!"

"You just did," her brother returned. "And I for one am shocked."

Proper or not, Constance hit his knee with her fan. "I did not. I wanted to know if Mr. Crawford believed what he said about acceptable choices."

"You are drawing attention, my dear," Aunt Gwladys cautioned. "You may fight properly in the carriage and again when we get home, but do try to refrain from doing so in public." She waited until she had gotten some indication from both Constance and Trefor that they would behave before turning back to the conversation Mrs. Barrett was having with Mr. Marsh.

Henry leaned closer to Constance and whispered his apology. "My mind was still on Mr. Edwards. I should have known you would not ask such a thing."

He paused to inhale the fragrance of roses that always surrounded her. It was quickly becoming his favourite fragrance. He would have to ask her what it was so that when he found a lady willing to marry him, he could purchase some for her.

He studied the lady sitting next to him. It really was too bad she was Linton's sister. For if she was not, he was almost certain he would request of her brother to call on her. Then again, if she was not Linton's sister, he would never have been allowed the opportunity to know her so well. She, like so many other proper young ladies, would have smiled politely at him, answered his questions with great civility, and never shown an ounce of preference for a gentleman with his reputation. Well, he supposed, that was not entirely correct. He was not without means, and there were proper chits that needed to make an advantageous marriage. In fact, he had thought that it might be best to start his quest for a bride with such ladies.

He leaned close to her again. "I do believe it." He shrugged when she looked his direction. "I understand the need to marry well and all that. However, I am enough of a sap to hope for marriage to be established on love if at all possible or mutual respect at the least."

Constance touched his arm quickly and lightly. There was a well of sorrow within the man next to her, and she knew it was not all from his rejection by Miss Price. "Your uncle's marriage was not such an arrangement, was it?" she asked softly.

He shook his head.

"That is unfortunate. My mother and father's marriage

was." One shoulder lifted and lowered in a half shrug. "I wish for such a marriage. I think many ladies do. Who does not wish to be respected?" Again she touched his arm. "Oh, I know there are those who prefer wealth and position, but I believe, if such a lady were to be honest with herself, she would admit that such things are empty. Why else would she go looking for ..." She clamped her lips closed and darted a look at her brother, who had cleared his throat.

Henry chuckled. He found the way Constance could get carried away by a topic and forget herself enough to trip over the thin line of propriety delightful. Sometimes her ideas would come out as a scold or, like now, as a passionate lecture as if she were instructing a room full of eager students.

She had lectured him on several things when they had toured the museum the other day, and, over the course of the last sennight, she had scolded him each and every time she thought he had forgotten to do something to his best ability. He had never had a more charming or alluring tutor. And his reward for having done as she expected — the sparkle in her eyes and the joy on her lips — was something he was beginning to crave.

He shot Linton a look of amusement. "I know I should not say it as it is highly improper, but I do know a thing or two about dissatisfied ladies, and you have the right of it."

Her cheeks grew rosy, and she lowered her gaze, just as

he knew she would. She only broached such topics when her mind was able in the passion of the moment to forget how improper a topic might be. However, when she was under good regulation, which she nearly always was, anything that even alluded to impropriety was met with the appropriate shock and embarrassment one would expect from a proper lady of delicate sensibilities.

Linton shook his head and rolled his eyes while a small smile touched his lips as the musicale was called to order. Henry breathed a sigh of relief. As much as he did not mind Constance's scolding, her brother's reprimand would be far less pleasant.

"Miss Foss plays very well, does she not?" Constance whispered in the pause between one lady leaving the piano and another arranging herself at her harp.

Henry nodded his agreement.

"And she is lovely and very proper." A strange flutter of something settled around Constance's heart. She had decided as she had sat in front of her mirror having her hair pinned into place, that it was time for her student to begin practising his skills on ladies that were not her and in situations that were not confined to dancing. She bit her lip as Henry agreed. She was most likely just nervous about sending her student out to be tested. She was not one who liked to fail, and should Henry fall short in any way, she would feel as if she had failed.

"You should approach her at the intermission," Constance suggested. "She is not being courted by anyone in particular even though her dowry is sizeable and her accomplishments nearly without fault. However, she is quiet and such reserve is somewhat off-putting to many gentlemen." She turned and smiled at him. "I know, you will succeed where others have not, for you are most amiable. Miss Foss will have no difficulty conversing with you."

"Is she dull?" Henry whispered as he turned his head to observe the lovely Miss Foss. She had a slight figure, not as well rounded as Constance's but pleasing, and her expression as she spoke to the older lady beside her was open and sincere.

"No, I have never found her to be," Constance replied. "However, I find fascination in things that others might not, so you will have to judge that for yourself."

"You are not dull." Henry shot her a smile, which was returned.

The first notes of the harp filled the room, and Constance touched her lips lightly, indicating that their conversation was over for the moment. The musician was proficient, and her song was beautiful, but Henry only half listened to it. His mind was otherwise occupied — first, in contemplation of how Constance's lips should feel if he were to place his finger on them, and then, by the unsettling knowledge that he would likely never know, both because her brother would kill him if he were to attempt to discover such a thing and because she seemed eager to have him on his way. Why else was she suggesting ladies to him? He knew that eventually, he would have to venture beyond the comfort of Constance's company, but he did not feel prepared to do so. In fact, his whole being clenched in aversion to the idea.

He leaned towards Constance. "Must I approach her tonight? Mightn't we just begin a list of options, and then I can begin another time?"

Again, she lay that finger on her lips.

"You do not know my preferences," he whispered.

Her brows furrowed with annoyance, and her lips pursed, but she made no other reply. She would not. During a performance was not the appropriate time to be speaking of such things — which Henry should know. Perhaps her student was not yet ready to present himself to best advantage among the sort of lady he claimed to be seeking. Maybe they should just discuss the possibilities and make a few introductions tonight. A child was not required to know how to read Shakespeare after a few lessons. He would be given time and opportunity to practice and improve. Perhaps that is what Henry needed — a gentle, considerate coaxing into society at large.

"Very well," she said, during the next break between musicians. "I will continue to point out those who I think are good choices, and Aunt Gwladys can make introductions as needed. Then tomorrow, we shall meet, and you can give me your list of preferences."

For the second time since he had sat down next to her this evening, Henry breathed a sigh of relief. This time, not because he feared her brother, but because he would not have to face being pushed out of her society for a while longer.

Chapter 6

Constance placed her pen in its holder and studied the list of five names before her. Each lady had seemed welcoming last night when Aunt Gwladys had introduced Henry to them, and although each chaperone had either raised a disapproving brow or given Henry an assessing look, his manners had seemed to win them over. He would likely not be turned away if he were to request a dance from or call on any of the ladies on this list. It was a good place to start. These ladies were all reserved and proper, which was what Henry had said he wanted during that first meeting when he had begged for her help.

She bit her lip and read the list again. Yes, they were all good candidates, all lovely young women, all friends and acquaintances of long standing. Each would make an excellent wife and mother. She should be delighted to have found five such possibilities for Henry, but she was not. She blew out a great breath and rose from the desk in the library before she succumbed to the odd desire to tear that list to shreds and toss it into the flames.

She paced a circuit around the room. Perhaps Henry's preferences would eliminate all of those ladies as options, she thought hopefully as she paused by the window and watched the people on the street below. A light rain was falling, so everyone was shuffling along much more quickly than normal. She rubbed her arms and turned back toward the fire. She would read a book until Henry's arrival. She could not think any longer about what sort of woman Henry needed as a wife. She had spent far too much time dwelling on that very thought instead of sleeping. She would wait to see what Henry's preferences were and then plan from there.

"Where are you off to this afternoon?" Linton asked as he entered the library.

"I am remaining at home today," Constance replied as she settled into a burgundy chair that wrapped around her.

Linton had crossed the room and was pulling a book from the shelf. "No outing with Crawford?" He glanced over his shoulder at her.

She shook her head. "No, he is calling here in a little less than an hour."

Her brother propped himself against a shelf and pretended to flip through the pages of his book. She knew he was not earnestly looking in the book, for his eyes were focused elsewhere — namely the floor in front of him.

"How many days has he called on you now?'

Constance tapped her fingers on her leg as she mentally listed off the things she had done with Henry since that first day he had appeared in her brother's drawing room looking for help. "If I count the ball where you insisted I dance with him, that would make today nine days that we have spent time together in one fashion or another." Nine, lovely days. She smiled softly and then sighed silently. Today might be their last for a while. Henry would likely call to let her know how things were progressing if she asked him to do so, but he would be driving other ladies through the park. Someone else would be on his arm as they toured the museum. The chair next to him at the theatre would be filled but not by her.

"I heard someone comment at my club this morning that Henry was courting you."

Constance looked up at her brother, who was still leaning against that shelf, holding his book in one hand but with his arms crossed. "And?" she prodded.

"I told them he was not courting you and that you were merely just friends."

She swallowed the sadness that rose in her throat at Trefor's comments and nodded her head. "That is true. Did they believe you?"

She knew how the ton worked. Once someone got an idea in their head, it was often hard to remove it. However, Henry's calling on other ladies would surely add veracity to what her brother had said.

Linton shrugged. "They seemed to, but one can never be too certain." He pushed off from the shelf and came to take a seat across from her. "It might be best to end your arrangement with him. I should hate for you not to have any other options present themselves because they believe you are already spoken for." He spoke gently and smiled as he placed a hand on her knee. "Remember, you have only one season before Aunt Gwladys begins arranging matches."

Constance forced a smile to her lips, though she could not seem to summon any actual amusement at the thought.

"Are you well?" Her brother asked, his brows furrowing in concern.

Constance nodded. It was a lie. She was not well. Her thoughts were a jumbled mess much like the yarn in her aunt's basket the last time Princess, their aunt's cat, had entertained herself with it.

"Are you certain?" He was still looking at her with that concerned expression.

Constance nodded again and then shook her head. She could not lie to her brother. It was not something she did.

"Is it Crawford?"

She blew out a breath. "I do not know what or who it is." She suspected it had something to do with Henry, but she could not say with perfect accuracy that he was the root of her muddled mind.

"You should end your agreement with him," her brother said firmly.

"I intend to," she replied. "That is why Aunt Gwladys introduced him to so many ladies last night. They are the beginning of a list of likely candidates for the role of Mrs. Crawford." Her heart pinched as she said it. "It is also why Mr. Crawford is calling today. We are going to go through the list and see which ones fit his preferences. Then, once I know more precisely what he is looking for in a wife, I can suggest other ladies to him." Oh, that thought made her wish to cry! She despised how weepy she became when overly tired.

"A list?" her brother asked curiously.

She tilted her head toward that rotten piece of paper. "It's on the desk."

Her brother rose and went to read it. "These are all good choices. Fine upstanding families and all that. None in need of a man of wealth."

Constance nodded her head. "I know. Well funded and proper. Perfect selections." She really should be more pleased with Henry's prospects, but the more she attempted to be, the more she wanted to fly back to her room and water her pillow with her tears for the next several hours. She should have told her maid that she was unwell this morning and stayed in bed. It was obvious that she was too tired for anyone's good.

"Three have sisters who have produced the required

heir in short order for their husbands, so Mr. Crawford should not need to worry on that account if he selects one of them."

Her brother peered over the paper at her. "I really wish you would find such topics less easy to discuss."

She smiled at him. "I assure you that I turn a brilliant shade of red if any such topic is discussed in my presence. However, I find that speaking to you does not cause me the same unease. So perhaps it is your fault."

He laughed. "I will not own that, but I am glad to hear you are not as willing to canvas such delicate topics with society as a whole." He placed the paper back on the desk. "You say Crawford will be here in less than an hour?"

"Half an hour, if the clock has been wound and is trustworthy," she replied.

"Well, then, I shall leave you to your reading while you wait." He paused at the door, turned, and gave her one last assessing look. "Would you allow him to court you if he asked?" He opened his mouth and closed it again. "I mean, has he improved so much as to be thought worthy of a proper chit's hand?"

Constance shrugged and nodded. "I believe he is. He likely still needs a bit of guidance as things are still new to him, but yes, I believe he is."

"Would you accept him? I mean if you liked him as more than a friend — not that I think you do," her brother stammered in a rather flustered fashion. "I am just attempting to gauge how much you think him improved."

Again she nodded. "I would."

"Then," her brother smiled, "well done."

"Thank you," she said as he turned to leave the room. At least one person thought that what she had accomplished in helping Henry was a good thing. Personally, with as scrambled as her thoughts were at the moment, she was not so certain that what she had done was anything less than dreadful.

~*~*~

Henry dashed from his carriage to the door of the Linton's townhouse. He knocked and then pulled his collar closer about his neck and tapped his hat down just a bit further. There was little he liked less on days like this than rain, cold rain, dripping down his back. Thankfully, Atkins was quick in answering the door, and Henry soon found himself relieved of his wet coat and hat and standing near the fire in the drawing room.

"Connie is in the library," Linton said as he entered the room. "She's reading while she waits for you. A tad early, are you not?" He wore a pleased smile.

Henry could well imagine why. He had not to this point in his life been known for his promptness. He had rather always preferred to arrive a few minutes past when he was expected. Time had never been his master, but rather he attempted to be the master of it – doing what he wished when he wished to do it. He took out his watch that had for years only been a decoration and looked at it. "I am only five minutes ahead of my time."

Linton chuckled. "Then have a seat and spend a few of those five minutes with me."

Henry sat in the chair his friend indicated.

"Your name came up at my club this morning," Linton began as he took a seat next to Henry.

Henry's brows rose. "I cannot imagine that I have done anything worthy of gossip. I have been spending my time most circumspectly."

Linton nodded. "Yes, that was one comment that was made. It seems your change in behaviour has not gone without notice." He crossed one ankle over the other. "Your attention to Connie has also not gone unnoticed. In fact, some were speculating that you had changed your behaviour to persuade me to accept you for her." He tilted his head and studied his friend. "Connie tells me that you have progressed to the point that I would not be wrong in accepting you as a possible suitor. I commend you on your success, of course, but I know that is not your design, and I said as much to the prattlers." He shrugged and shook his head. "I am not sure if the busybodies will heed my words or not, and I cannot say I am not a little worried that Connie's options for making a match will not be hindered by such talk."

Henry's heart sank. He did not wish to harm Constance

in any fashion — not purposefully or accidentally. "I had worried my being seen with her might cause some unpleasantness. I said so on our first drive."

Linton nodded. "Yes, I know. Connie said as much." He paused, his lips pressed together. "I think it best if you were to distance yourself from her for a time. Be seen with others, that sort of thing."

Again, Henry's heart sank. "Of course," he agreed. What else could he do?

Linton rose. "I am happy you understand. It is not you that I am opposed to, it is just that Connie needs to find a match eventually, but she will hide behind whatever she can to put it off."

Henry nodded and pushed out of his chair.

"I understand she has a list of possible candidates for you," Linton continued. "All very good prospects."

"Yes, they seemed very nice when I met them last night." He had not found one that had interested him to any great extent, but it was a place to start. His estate needed an heir after all, and marrying was the only way to procure one. He followed Linton down the hall and to the library.

"Connie, Crawford is here. Shall I send for Aunt Gwladys or your maid?"

Constance snapped her book closed and stuffed her feet into her slippers quickly. "My maid. I fear Aunt Gwladys would have too many helpful ideas," she said as she stood and straightened her skirts. She had meant to tuck her feet up under her and settle into the chair comfortably to read. However, her tired eyes would not cooperate, and she had eventually nodded off.

"Very well. I shall have your maid sent to you directly."

"Thank you," she called to the back of her brother.

"How are you today, Mr. Crawford?" she asked with what she hoped was a bright smile.

"I am well despite the weather," he replied.

"It is a rather damp day, is it not?" she asked as she went to the desk to retrieve her list of names. "Much better suited to staying in bed with a good book and a cup of tea than being out and about."

"Indeed," he replied, his mind wandering to the image of Constance tucked up in bed. He shook his head — such thoughts would not do. He was not that man any longer. He pulled his list from his pocket. "I think I have listed all of the things I prefer a lady to be," he said as he joined her in front of the fire.

She put out her hand, and he placed his list in it and then pulled a chair next to hers so that they could both read the lists she held.

"As you can see, I divided it into character qualities and physical attributes. Obviously, the character qualities will be of greater concern."

"A gentleman does not want a dowdy wife any more than a lady wishes for a stodgy husband," Constance said with a smile. "As long as we are agreed that a lady's appearance, though pleasant, is not so important as how she will treat you, your estate, and your children." Her gaze fell to the pages she held. His children. One of these ladies might just be the one that would call Everingham home and be the mother of Henry's children. She blew out a breath.

"Are you well?" he asked in concern.

"This is a grave responsibility," she replied. "I would not wish for my guidance to leave you with an unhappy future." Even if it would likely leave her with one. Oh, she should have listened to her brother's warning, she suddenly realized. Just because you do not plan to fall in love or have your heart broken does not mean those things will not happen.

Henry placed a hand on her arm. "You are not forcing me to accept any of your suggestions. My happiness lies firmly in my own possession."

She gave him a grateful smile. "Then shall we proceed?" Her eyes scanned his list. He had such fine penmanship for a gentleman. It was easily read, neat, and precise with a small flourish here and there. It seemed very fitting, considering his charming personality. "Not a fortune hunter. Someone who wishes to love and be loved. Not a constant talker. Soft and gentle manners. Not brash. Knows her own mind. Would be happy in town equally as much as in the country." She looked up at him. "You have not listed which accomplishments she should possess. Music? Painting? Dancing?"

He chuckled. "I do like to dance, so I suppose we could include that, but the rest are of very little use in determining the value of a lady. They are but accoutrements to garner attention. " He looked at the shelf behind her. "Reading. I would prefer a wife who enjoys reading. Ladies who abhor the activity are usually flighty and annoyingly talkative."

She inclined her head in acceptance of the fact. "Yes, they tend to be less intelligent, too, which is likely not a good quality for a mother or the mistress of an estate. Such tasks require some amount of cleverness."

She studied the names of the ladies on her list. "Miss Foss can dance well, but I know she is not fond of it. Shall I remove her name?"

"No, just make a notation, if you would. I might need to be flexible in some areas."

"Very well," she made a note next to Miss Foss's name. "Hmm, I think Miss Alberts has no marks against her." Unfortunately. "And neither do Miss Bellamy or Miss Norwood, but Miss Royce is also not fond of dancing, nor does she attend our book readings or ever enter into a discussion about books or poetry. I cannot say for certain that she does not read, but, well, without being impolite, she is not excessively clever. She is incredibly sweet, just not clever." She glanced at him. "Do I make a note or cross her off."

"A note," he replied. He needed enough ladies to be

seen with to keep a possible attachment to any one particular lady from becoming the topic of gossip.

Drat. Her nose wrinkled as she jotted down the information. "You have seen each of these ladies. Are there any that you wish to remove from the list based on appearance?"

All of them. He wished to eliminate all of them. He did not want to be sent out to search for a wife rather than calling on Constance.

"No," he replied. "They do not meet my ideals, but that does not mean they are not worthy of a chance. A lady's heart is more important than the colour of her eyes or the turn of her nose."

"Do you mean it?"

"Yes, I do. I have learned how important a lady's disposition is. A figure will soften, wrinkles will etch a face, hair will turn white, but a good heart shall remain a good heart."

Despite her best efforts not to do so, Constance sighed. "That is beautiful," she whispered. "Some lady will be very lucky to have you."

"Do you mean it? Do you approve of me?" He held his breath as he awaited her response.

She nodded as she looked at his anxious face. "I do." She held his gaze for one heartbeat longer and then turned her eyes back to his list. "If I am to make proper suggestions, I should know what sort of appearance you prefer."

He leaned toward her and covered that section of the paper with his hand, causing her to turn eyes the perfect shade of blue up at him. "You do not need to read this now."

"But I want to know." It was not a lie. She was curious to see if any of the five ladies she had listed met his ideals of feminine beauty.

"Then let me tell you." Being so close to her was intoxicating. He drew a deep breath. "She must smell like roses," he began with a smile. "And have light eyes." He stroked a finger gently near the corner of her eye. "A small nose." He tapped hers and added with a grin, "and it mustn't be hooked."

"What of her hair?" Constance flushed at the breathy sound of her voice.

"Brown, not too dark, and not too light." He slid his fingers along a tendril that hung loose in front of her ear. "Cheeks that glow sweetly just as yours are doing right now." He lay a hand on her cheek. "A figure that is not as slight as Miss Floss's or as rounded as Miss Bellamy's." His finger touched her lips. "Soft lips that smile easily." He ran his finger along her bottom lip, his eyes following its path. His head bent towards her. How he wished to kiss those lips! But this was Linton's sister. He must not steal a kiss — no matter how much he desired it.

"Forgive me," he whispered, pulling his hand away from her and straightening. "I forgot myself in your loveliness."

He rose and pulled the list of ladies' names from her lap. "I shall approach each of these ladies before I return." He folded the paper. "Two weeks should be plenty of time, I should think." He bowed. "Thank you, Miss Linton. You have been a great help," he said and, then, turned and hurried from the room.

Chapter 7

Henry dashed down the steps of the Linton townhouse and barely had the patience to wait for the door to his carriage to be opened for him.

What had he been thinking? Admiring her? Touching her? Almost kissing her? He shook his head and then allowed it to drop into his hands as he leaned his elbows on his knees. Foolish, foolish, foolish!

He could feel the water dripping from the brim of his hat and tossed the offending item to the bench across from him.

How had he thought he could change enough to treat a lady worthy of honour in a fashion in which she deserved to be treated?

He pulled the list of ladies she had made for him from his pocket. None of these ladies deserved to be tied to a man such as he. One moment of temptation — the presence of a beguiling and beautiful woman with the smile and heart of an angel — and he was undone. Hopeless. He was utterly hopeless.

The remainder of the drive to his home was spent in remonstrating himself and pointing out his weaknesses. So effective was his self-deprecation that by the time he had entered his own library, he wished only for a large bottle of fiery liquid — the fierier, the better — to burn from his memory the image of lips parted slightly, wide blue eyes watching him as he spoke, and breasts rising and falling as her breathing slowed and deepened. She was not a lonely wife or a bored widow. She was an innocent — a respectable, virtuous lady. He crumpled the list she had given him and tossed it into the fire. It would be better for one and all if he once again locked up his heart and went back to pleasing himself as his uncle taught him.

He filled a glass with something from his cabinet, took a large swallow, poured enough in to replace that swallow, and then went to the writing table. His sister no doubt had some friends who needed a charming fellow to tickle their ears with flattery and who would handsomely reward him for his efforts. He paused for a moment before dipping his pen in ink and applying it to paper. He drained half of what was in his glass in an attempt to rid himself of the imagined disappointment he saw on a fair face. He closed his eyes and shook his head. At least it was no longer Fanny reproving him for doing what he knew he ought not. His hand trembled ever so slightly as he dipped his pen and began to write a letter to his sister, speaking of his boredom and inquiring if there was any function she knew of that might help remedy such a tiresome state. His foray into propriety had been no more than a lark, and not even a very enjoyable one. He drained the last of his glass and signed his name with a flourish. He would send it tomorrow.

Rising, he went to refill his drink and retired with it and the bottle to the chairs before the fire, removing his boots and stripping down to his shirt and breeches before flopping into his favourite chair and proceeding to drink far more than he knew he should, but he did not care. If he could but rid his mind of her face, her smell, her...just her, then he might be able to send that admission of failure to his sister tomorrow.

Tomorrow came in all its painful brilliance as the sun drove the rain away. Henry moaned and scrubbed his face. His stomach roiled, joining his head in rebuking him for his actions. Rising, he stretched his stiff limbs and back. His eyes fell on that letter he had written. He should send it. He should just admit his defeat. But he could not. Not yet. If he sent it now, Mary would be on his doorstep in an hour if not sooner, and he did not wish to see anyone at present. What he wished for now was something to help settle his stomach, a bath, and his bed. There was no need to consign himself to his unhappy fate while feeling as if a coach and six had driven over him. He rubbed his forehead between his eyes and slowly made his way from the library to find someone to get whatever it was that he needed.

The sun had set, and the moon had taken its place when Henry finally stirred a second time. He rose from his bed and padded to the fire to give it a stir. He tugged his robe more closely about him and lifted the clock off the mantle so that he could squint at it through scratchy, blurry eyes to see what time it was. Midnight? He blinked and squinted at the clock once again. Yes, it did say midnight. He held it to his ear. It was ticking as it should be. He gave the mechanism a winding and replaced the clock on the mantle.

His stomach rumbled. It was too late to rouse someone to bring him a plate of food, so he lit his candle and went in search of some cold meat or cheese and bread. And tea, he told himself. Tea was all he was going to drink tonight, even if that persistent vision of a fair face continued to occupy every corner of his mind.

Half an hour later, having searched the kitchen as quietly as he was able and only waking one servant, he was on his way back to his room, tray of food in hand and was about to climb the stairs when that letter seemed to call to him from the library. Deciding he should retrieve it, he turned, placed his tray on a hall table and went in search of that distasteful piece of paper. Then, having retrieved it, he returned to his room to eat and contemplate his future.

As he ate, Henry read and reread his letter to Mary. Each

time he got to the end, he shook his head and sighed. This. This empty existence of seeking pleasure was not for what he wished. What he wanted was a wife and a family — not as he had experienced — a real family with a father who taught his son properly and a wife he loved and loved him in return. How his sister would laugh to hear such talk from him! It was rather maudlin after all. He drank the last of his tea and tossed his letter into the fire.

He had been at this point before — faced with temptation and a choice to chose ease over responsibility. He had not chosen wisely that time and what had its reward been? A well-deserved broken heart. That would not happen this time. This time he would choose the correct path.

He picked up his candle and made his way down the stairs once again. This time he traveled to see what invitations might be lying on his desk. There must be at least one which might provide him with the opportunity to meet one of the ladies Constance had placed on that list. He had no intention, however, of falling in love with any of them, but he could not return to Constance before he had done as he said he would.

He would be seen with several other ladies. He would make an attempt to be the perfect gentleman, and perhaps in so doing, he would prove himself worthy of the one lady he heard in his thoughts, saw in his dreams, and doubted he could eradicate from his heart.

~*~*~

"I see Mr. Crawford is accompanied by Miss Foss this evening," Aunt Gwladys whispered behind her fan to Constance. "That is three of the four ladies from your list with whom we have seen him." Her eyes searched her niece's face.

Constance had been less lively than normal over the past week. She had attended soirees and taken a walk or two with her friend Evelyn, but she had done so without so much as a protest. It really was not like her to be led about in society from function to function unless it was something that had to do with poetry or science or some other bookish thing. Not one function over the past week had even hinted at broadening the intellect until tonight's play. She had not even protested being introduced to gentlemen of her aunt's choosing, and Aunt Gwladys was beginning to worry about her.

She was not eating as heartily as she was wont to do; she withdrew to her room or the library as often as she could, and her maid had mentioned that many mornings her mistress had risen with red eyes and required resting with a compress before she exited her room.

Constance drew a breath and released it quietly. Two more ladies to go and then Henry would return to her. She blinked against the dampness that rose in her eyes. She must not let anyone know how much she missed him or wished to be seated next to him in his box. Her aunt might understand the constant ache that resided in Constance's heart, but her brother had threatened Henry, and if Trefor suspected that Henry had caused her to be unhappy, he might feel it his duty to follow through on his threat.

"Miss Foss appears to be enjoying herself," she forced a smile to her lips and attempted to feel it enough that it would shine somewhat in her eyes. "I told Mr. Crawford that his amiable ways would help her to be less reserved." She turned her eyes back to the box across from them. "He is doing very well."

She should be happy that she had succeeded in helping him find his footing in society as he had wished. However, she was not. Last evening, at the Henderson's ball, he had been very popular with the ladies standing at the side watching the dancing. She had heard many of their whispers about his fine form and lightness of foot. More than one had hinted that she would be delighted to have him call on her. And Constance had longed to trip each and every one of them.

"He has not singled out any in particular, however," her aunt continued, keeping her fan in front of her lips. It was too easy for a conversation to be read by those intent on doing so. "Perhaps in time."

"Yes," Constance agreed. "Perhaps." Eventually, it would happen. She knew it would. If only it could be her. If only he could sit so closely to her again and touch her as he had that day in the library. She was almost certain he had forgotten himself and had not just been toying with her — she was *almost* certain. If only she could see him and speak to him for more than just a greeting, she would know, would she not?

"I see Mr. Upton is here unaccompanied." Her aunt turned toward Linton. "We could encounter him at the intermission or the end, do you not think?"

"Aunt," Constance begged. "Not tonight. Just let me enjoy a play without having to be paired with someone."

Her aunt brushed the request aside. "Nonsense. A brief meeting would not be so dreadful."

Constance sighed. "Very well. Where shall we conduct this clandestine affair?"

"Clandestine, indeed!" huffed her aunt.

"We will take a walk and find some refreshment," said Linton. "Nothing unusual to such a thing."

There were a few other suggestions from her aunt to her brother about unattached gentlemen that they might be able to meet by chance while walking. Constance did not continue to listen. It did not matter whom they happened upon, for she was certain her heart was not in the condition needed to be interested in any of them.

How she longed to just be gone from town! A respite in the country would be just the thing to refresh her and prepare herself for whatever future lay before her, and then next season, she would return ready to have her aunt present matches and to help her brother accept the best offer.

"Are you well?" her brother asked.

Constance blinked and turned toward him. "I apologize. I was merely thinking of home and how a walk in the garden would be so refreshing." She tipped her head and pulled her lip between her teeth. "Do you suppose we might return home before the season ends? Must we stay for all of it?"

"We shall do no such thing, and you certainly must," Aunt Gwladys answered before her nephew could. "You will never find a good match in the country. All the gentlemen of value are in town."

Constance sighed. "It is just so tiring — all these late nights and activities."

Her brother guffawed. "Tiring? To you?" He shook his head. "You shall have to devise a better excuse than that." He wore a smirk as he looked her fully in the face. "Unless you are truly unwell. Then we can consult a physician."

Constance's eyes grew wide. She disliked medical examinations and treatments of any kind. "I am well, but I am tired. This season has been disappointing." That was the truth. Let him do with it what he would. She would not engage with him further — probably.

"Due to your lack of participation," Linton muttered. "The only thing you have thrown yourself into since we arrived is this project with Crawford."

"I like helping people. Projects are entertaining." She snapped her mouth closed, once again determined to ignore her brother.

"Then make a dress or a hat," grumbled her brother.

"Miss Barrett seems rather taken with Mr. Marsh. You could help her by planning a dinner as a dinner party would be very entertaining. We could invite several young ladies and a few gentlemen. We could have music and perhaps a dramatic reading." Aunt Gwladys clapped her hands in delight at her scheme.

Linton scowled but allowed that it was not a completely dreadful idea.

"You do know that some of the young ladies she will invite will be there for you," Constance said to her brother with a laugh.

"Some?" her aunt agreed with a smile. "I would like to see the next generation of Lintons before I turn up my toes."

"Oh, Aunt," Constance said with a great deal of emotion, "you are far from being ready for the grave. There are many years yet before you must worry about such a thing."

Aunt Gwladys patted Constance's hand where it lay on her arm. "As quickly as you two are moving toward marriage, I most certainly must worry about it. Now if one or the other of you would show some inclination to the marital state, I might rest easy, but as it is, I cannot."

Constance gave her aunt a sad smile. "I am sorry. If I could..."

Her aunt patted her hand again. "You will find the right one. Who knows. You may have already met him and just do not yet realize it." A shadow of something passed across her niece's face, causing the light in Constance's eyes to fade. She leaned closer to her niece's ear. "Or perhaps you do realize it?"

Constance shook her head and glanced at her brother.

"I am quite certain your brother is incapable of killing anyone; however," she whispered and then tapped her lip with her finger to indicate that Constance's secret was safe with her.

Chapter 8

"Henry," Mary slipped an arm through her brother's as she came up beside him. "I do believe you have danced with half the wallflowers in the last week and a half. Surely, you could find better partners than that."

"Good evening, Mary." Henry spared her a quick glance.

"What? You are not going to defend your decline in taste of partners?" She laughed lightly.

"No." He had no desire to enter into any extended conversation with his sister about whom he did or did not choose as a dance partner.

"You are becoming a great bore."

He kept his eyes forward, but he could well imagine the pout that accompanied such a tone. "Being respectable is not the same as becoming a bore."

She once again laughed. "Respectable is so dull." She sighed. "I did not come over here to argue with you about your recent disturbing behaviour, nor did I come to scold you for the way you spoke to me the last time we met — although I should, you know."

"I know nothing of the sort."

She made that particular sound in her throat as if holding back a huff, the sound that very clearly let him know that she was not pleased with him.

"What do you truly wish, Mary?"

"You are missed by our friends. Can you not accept just one invitation to a soiree from me?"

He knew the hurt in her voice was affected. He had heard her do it many times over when attempting to get what she desired. Still, it tugged at his heart.

"You know I cannot. If I am seen in the same company as I was before the incident with Mrs. Rushworth, my chances of securing the kind of wife for which I wish will be greatly diminished." He turned toward her and smiled. "You could join my company. I may be able to secure you an invitation to any soiree to which I am invited."

"I should think not! I do not wish to be thought of as dull."

"You could never be dull, my dear sister. You shine no matter the circumstances in which you find yourself." He patted the hand that still held his arm. "Do you not wish for a happy marriage? You will not find it amongst your friends. There is not a one of them that is content." His mouth tipped up in a roguish smile. "I can assure you of the correctness of that fact if you wish."

She feigned shock at his comments just as he knew she

would. "I shall find an acceptable marriage and all that goes along with it."

"Houses, carriages, money, lovers? Really, Mary? You would wish to have such a life?"

She shrugged. "It is the way of things. What you are chasing is an illusion. You will find a girl to please you for a time, but then another shall come along and you will realize that the same porridge every day is not satisfying. That is just how it is."

He shook his head. "No, I do not accept that."

"Accepted or not, it is what it is, Henry. Now, tell me, which of these lovely ladies has captured the once charming and adventurous Mr. Crawford? Is it she in the pink with the dark hair and generous curves? Or perhaps the tall blonde in the lavender?"

He patted her hand again and then lifted it from his arm as he chuckled. "You shall know at the wedding breakfast. Until then, you must guess just as everyone else must."

His eyes caught sight of Constance and followed her for a distance as she circled the ballroom with her aunt. "I must go. I have someone waiting for me for the next set." He bowed and left her.

He had only one lady, Miss Alberts, left on his list. He must dance with her tonight and call on her tomorrow. Then, after a day of impatient waiting, he would once again be able to call on Constance and report to her that none of her recommendations had captured his heart.

After which, he intended to see if he could determine whether he had any hope of ever winning her. If he did, he would go to her brother and suffer whatever punishment Linton might level at him for having fallen in love with Constance. A broken nose, a bloodied lip, a bullet in his shoulder, a year of confinement to his estate, it did not matter; he would bear any or all of it if Constance loved him.

"Miss Alberts," he said with a bow as he approached her. "I believe this is our dance."

He schooled his features to not show his surprise at the snort that accompanied her small giggle as she accepted his hand.

~*~*~

"Henry refuses every attempt."

Constance casually looked to her right and then, with just as much nonchalance, turned to her left and the source of the comment. Miss Crawford stood next to some lady in blue. Constance attempted to recall her name. She was certain she had either met her or at least heard her name in some conversation. Miss Crawford's friend was familiar looking, but try as she might, Constance could not bring the lady's name to mind.

"You told him he was a bore?"

"I did. He said he is not a bore but rather he is respectable."

Both ladies laughed at that.

"Henry shall never truly be respectable. He may play the part for a while — even long enough to get one of those milquetoast maids to accept him."

How could his sister speak about him in such a fashion! Henry was capable of being respectable. It was not an act, but a desire of his heart. Constance had seen that desire in his eyes as he listened and attempted to do all the things she asked of him.

"He has been on the verge of being lost to respectability before," Miss Crawford's companion said. "It was fortunate that he was not so stuffy then as he is now and did not cut us off."

"Yes, well, that did not work out as well as it should have."

Miss Crawford's friend chuckled. "Who was to know that in all of England you found the one man of the cloth who was devoted to it so completely."

"I should rather like to forget Mr. Bertram and his wife," Mary retorted.

Constance saw Mr. Delaney coming to claim her for the next dance and prepared herself to accept him with what appeared to be eagerness. Her aunt knew that she hoped for another gentleman to claim her hand eventually, but her brother did not, and Constance preferred to keep it that way as long as she could.

"Now, about your brother," said Miss Crawford's

friend. "It would be such a blow to lose him forever from our group. He is such a pleasure to have at a party."

Constance's eyes grew slightly wide at the tone of voice the woman used. An innocent she might be, but she was not naive and knew enough to recognize innuendo when she heard it.

"A rendezvous in the garden would not ruin my night," the lady in blue continued, "although it might ruin your brother's chances to make the sort of match he seems determined to make. Do you think you could get him to walk with you?"

"Miss Linton," Mr. Delaney greeted her with a small bow.

Constance curtseyed and took his hand, glancing back over her shoulder as he led her out onto the dance floor. Miss Crawford was still standing there talking to her friend. Constance would have to keep an eye on them and try to find a way to warn Henry. No one was going to take away his chance to find the happiness he sought if she could find a way to prevent it.

"Are you looking for someone in particular?" Mr. Delaney did not seem particularly impressed by Constance's scanning of the ballroom as they lined up and waited for the music to begin.

"No, I am just taking it all in," she lied. She had hoped to see Henry among the gentlemen of this set, but he was not here. He was somewhere else and in danger of falling prey to whatever scheme his sister and her friend had hatched. However, not wishing to offend her partner any further, Constance turned her attention back to the group of which they were a part.

"The candles make everything fairly sparkle, do they not?" she asked Mr. Delaney, earning a smile from the gentleman.

"And the decor," Constance continued. "Such flower arrangements! I dare say it is the most beautifully decorated ball I have been to yet this season."

The gentleman across from her shrugged. "I do not find it any more exceptional than most," he replied. "But then I am a gentleman and such things do not always catch our attention the way they do for a lady. Ladies are far better suited for noticing such things. It is part of their delicate nature, I suppose."

"I suppose," Constance agreed. His slightly condescending tone grated. It appeared Mr. Delaney was not the sort of gentleman to think highly of ladies. He would definitely not do as a suitor.

She allowed her eyes to wander down the line of dancers as she asked, "Do you like art?"

The music began as her eyes fell on a person who might be of some use in protecting Henry — if she could just get him to think of something other than himself for a moment.

Mr. Delaney spoke at length — broken as their conversation was by the steps of the dance — about art and what he thought constituted a great artist. It came as no surprise to Constance that the man preferred scenes of hunting and sport to those that featured softer objects such as flowers and pastoral scenes.

Constance did her best to keep the conversation going without arguing too often with him over what truly made a piece of art captivating. She worked her way through the steps and turns of the dance. Finally, the pattern placed her where she wanted to be.

"Mr. Edwards," she said quickly as they joined hands, "I have need of your assistance."

His brows rose. "How so?" he asked before they parted.

A few steps later, she was once again near enough to speak to him. "I am going to the retiring room after this dance."

They were parted for a moment. There was but one more chance to speak to him before the figure would return her to Mr. Delaney.

"There is an alcove just past it. Meet me there."

A roguish grin curled his lips.

She shook her head and scowled lightly at him as he moved away.

He shrugged but gave a nod of his head.

For the remainder of the dance, she split her attention between her partner and trying to find either Henry or his sister in the people standing about but could not. It was with a great sigh of relief that she made her final curtsey and was returned to her aunt's side.

"Mr. Delaney cuts a fine figure," her aunt commented as the man departed from them.

"His figure may be fine, Aunt, but his intellect is wanting."

Aunt Gwladys chuckled softly at the comment. "You are a very strange sort of girl, my dear. Most would only wish for a handsome husband with a handsome bank account."

"Well, I wish for both of those as well as a handsome mind," Constance replied with a smile. "Now, I really must go freshen myself," she whispered behind her fan.

"Can it not wait. Mr. Emerson was asking after you. He might return."

"No, it cannot wait. I will not be long." She held her breath, hoping that her aunt would allow her to go alone. Providence must have heard her plea, for just as her aunt looked about to say she would accompany her, Mrs. Barrett, wearing a very pleased smile approached, and Aunt Gwladys suggested that Evelyn accompany Constance.

Constance linked arms with her dear friend and pulled her close as they walked. "I am going to meet someone after we have visited the retiring room," she whispered.

Evelyn's eyes grew wide. "A gentleman?"

Constance nodded. "Mr. Edwards."

Evelyn gasped.

"I need his help." Constance leaned closer and whispered to her friend all she had heard pass between Miss Crawford and the lady in blue.

"How dreadful," Evelyn said as they entered the retiring room. "I will go with you to meet with Mr. Edwards."

Constance gave her friend's hand a grateful squeeze before they parted to attend to their needs.

~*~*~

Constance held on to Evelyn's arm tightly as the two of them slipped behind the curtain that hung in front of the alcove. She was certain her heart had never beaten so quickly or as loudly as it was at this moment. To be found in an alcove with a gentleman such as Mr. Edwards would do neither her nor Evelyn any good. Her brother had cautioned her on many occasions that Mr. Edwards was only to be spoken to in the light of day and in a public place. Otherwise, she was to be standing next to her brother while conversing with the man. Apparently, the rumors that circulated about him among the young ladies were not as fanciful as she had at first assumed. The man was a rake of the first order.

"I was beginning to think you were not coming," Edwards said with a smile.

"I told you I was going to the retiring room — which I did." She was surprised at how her voice did not betray the unease she felt. "Now, we only have five minutes." She huffed as she saw his eyes taking in the length of her friend. "Mr. Edwards, please, if I could have your attention."

He turned his eyes back to her. "Are you not going to introduce me to your friend?" he asked.

Constance's eyes narrowed and one brow rose as her lips pursed in displeasure. "No," she replied, "I am not. If you wish to be introduced to my friend, you must do so through a proper channel." She lowered her voice just a bit. "My brother has told me the sort of man you are, sir. I will not subject my friend to knowing you because of my actions."

Edwards chuckled. "Linton warned you about me, did he?"

"Many times," Constance replied.

"Then why have you not stayed away? I was under the impression that you were a very proper chit."

Constance smiled. "I am. However, I am also an intelligent chit."

His brows rose at her use of the word chit.

"And," she continued, "you have just the reputation and skills I require."

Chapter 9

"You will not hate me for having told him your name, will you?" Constance asked Evelyn for the third time since they had left the alcove.

"It is not as if he left you a choice," Evelyn replied. "Besides, he already knew my name. He spoke to us at the musicale, remember?"

Constance's brows furrowed. She clearly remembered him talking to them about Mr. Marsh. "Then why was he insistent on my introducing you?" Some gentlemen were so vexingly difficult to understand.

Evelyn shrugged. "Most likely because he could. You refused to do so when we first entered the alcove, and then he saw an opportunity to force you to do what you did not want to do. Has your brother not ever behaved in such a fashion? Mine has. He will often try to make me do things I have refused to do — nothing heinous or truly disgusting, but little things. Once he wished for me to give him my dessert. I refused because it was almond cake, and you know how I love almond cake. So does he." She gave

Constance a pointed look. "However, he also knew that I wished for a bit more pin money to buy a hat. I had something he wanted, and he had something I wanted."

"That does not seem to be the same."

Evelyn shrugged again. "Perhaps it is not precisely the same, but some gentlemen prefer to make bargains rather than cast their help about in a charitable fashion."

Constance frowned. She was not positive Evelyn was correct, but she could not, with any certainty, refute the argument either. So, she let it stand.

"Do you wish to walk in the garden?" Evelyn asked. "I think some fresh air might be just the thing for the headache I am planning to develop."

Constance enjoyed it when her friend got that mischievous glint in her eyes as she had now. Evelyn might be all that was proper and demure when she was supposed to be, but Constance knew that behind her friend's mannerly exterior lay a heart which craved the occasional adventure.

"I would not wish to be the cause of your discomfort," Constance replied. "But do you suppose your mother and my aunt will allow us to walk unattended?"

A scowl touched Evelyn's lips. "Would your brother go with us?"

"Trefor?" Constance squeaked.

"He would be less of a hindrance than my mother," Evelyn said quietly. "He would walk quietly and not suggest at which gentlemen I should or should not smile."

Constance could understand how her friend felt. Her aunt was little better. To Mrs. Barrett and Aunt Gwladys, the season seemed to be a great, fun game of strategy. For those, such as herself and Evelyn, who were the game pieces, it was far less exciting.

"Very well," Constance agreed. "But Trefor must not know that I spoke to Mr. Edwards or about how I feel about Mr. Crawford."

Evelyn squeezed her friend's arm tightly. "You truly love him?"

"I do." Constance shrugged. "I did not mean to love him, but I do. He is not the sort of gentleman for whom I wished. His reputation is not so sparkling as I would like, and although I believe him capable of being faithful, I will not lie and say I have not questioned his ability to remain so. Yet, I love him." She turned questioning eyes to Evelyn. "Am I wrong to wish to marry him?"

Evelyn shook her head. "No. My mother was just yesterday commenting on how improved he was. She even said she would not be opposed to having him call on me — although she already knows I am not the sort of lady he would prefer since he said so when we met him at your house. " Evelyn leaned a little closer to Constance and spoke even more quietly as they made their way through the people standing on the edges of the ballroom. "And, you said he has refused his sister's offers of whatever many times, did you not? I think that in and of itself proves he is a different person if his sister fears he has become properly dull. Do you not agree?"

Constance could not argue that point.

"And you believe him capable of being all he should be, do you not?" Evelyn continued.

"I do. With my whole heart, I do."

"Then you are not wrong to wish as you do," she whispered softly as they were nearly next to Constance's brother. "Mr. Linton," she said raising her voice, "I feel a bit of a headache starting and would very much like to take some air. Would you be so kind as to accompany your sister and me on a short walk? I should hate to take my mother away from your aunt."

He looked to his aunt. "Would that be acceptable? I do not wish to take your charge away from you when there are all those gentlemen with whom she has not yet danced."

Constance nearly laughed at the scowl on her aunt's face. Her brother was not the most patient sort of person when it came to listening to his aunt and her friend discuss matchmaking as it often led to recommendations about his own need of a bride. And from her aunt's reply, she guessed that the conversation had taken such a turn.

"I am more worried about it taking you away from your duty to find a wife," his aunt muttered.

"There might be a lovely lady in the garden," he

returned. "One that likes dancing as much as I do," he added sardonically.

Constance chuckled. Her brother did not truly mind dancing. He just disliked being required to dance with this or that lady since she would, in his aunt's opinion, make a wonderful Mrs. Linton.

"If a lady is hiding in the garden..."

"May I go for a walk?" Constance interrupted before her aunt could begin a lecture on what constituted a proper lady. "Please?"

"Very well, but do not be gone long. Gentlemen who are hiding in the garden are not the sort of men that make good husbands." She gave a pointed look to Linton. "Those of any worth are in the ballroom."

"Or at home," Linton muttered as he led his sister and Evelyn toward the terrace door. "I love her, but I truly wish she would let me be. I can find my own wife."

"And I can find my own husband," said Constance.

"As can I," agreed Evelyn.

"As long as you find him this season, my dear sister, for you know her plans if you do not," Linton warned as they stepped out into the night.

~*~*~

Edwards strolled the paths of the garden seeking his quarry. How he had allowed himself to be talked into saving a friend from the clutches of a willing woman, he would never know. It was not as if he was the charitable sort. He smiled. There. Leaning against a tree in the shadows. It was not a lady in a blue dress, but it was the friend he needed to save. This mission should be over quickly. Then, he could be on his way back inside where he was certain a game of cards and some poor chap's money were awaiting him.

"Crawford," he called as he drew closer. "Are you alone?"

"As you can see," Henry returned.

"Did you come out here with your sister?" Edwards took up a piece of tree trunk next to his friend and affected the same easy pose Henry wore.

"I came out here to avoid her," Henry replied. "She has been at my heels all night." He turned toward Edwards. "Why? Are you looking for her?"

Edwards shook his head. "No, I was looking for you and some lady in blue."

"I beg your pardon?"

Edwards shrugged. "Linton's sister and her friend Miss Barrett cornered me and persuaded me to help them find you and save you from having your reputation ruined by some lady in blue. Apparently, neither lady was concerned with my reputation being ruined." He wore a wide grin.

There were several questions that Edwards's explanation raised in Henry's mind. But the most pressing one was
—

"How, precisely, did they persuade you?" The question

rumbled from Henry, for he knew that his friend was not known for bestowing favours without expecting one in return.

Edwards chuckled. "You nearly growled that as well as Linton would. I do believe you have left me to be the only disreputable one among our group."

"How?" Henry rumbled again.

Edwards shrugged. "Miss Linton asked, and I obliged."

"Just like that?"

Edwards blew out a breath. He had surprised himself with how easily he had capitulated to her request. He had thought to demand at least a kiss for his service — not from Linton's sister — he did not have a death wish — but from her friend. He smiled at the thought of those perfectly pink lips. Those were lips he wished to taste at some point. "I made her introduce her friend."

"Miss Barrett? Did you not already know her?"

"I did. Although when they entered the alcove, I did not recognize her at first and then when Miss Linton refused to introduce her, I felt compelled to make her give the introduction."

"You were in an alcove with Miss Barrett and Miss Linton?"

Edwards nodded. "The one just down from the ladies' retiring room. The one where Miss Linton told me to meet her."

"Oh, for heaven's sake, begin at the beginning and tell

me how you came to be here," Henry growled. Why would Constance be asking Edwards to meet her in an alcove!

"Do you like her?"

"Do I like whom?"

"Linton's sister."

"Yes. Now, tell me how you came to be here."

"Yes?" The question was accompanied by a short, surprised burst of laughter.

"Yes," Henry repeated. "I love her."

Again, Edwards laughed. "Does Linton know?"

"No, and you are not to tell either him or her."

Edwards smiled broadly. "You have not told Miss Linton you love her?"

Henry shook his head.

"Well, it should come as some relief to you then that I suspect your feelings are returned. Oh, ho! Linton is going to be beside himself when he finds out."

"But he will not find out from you." Henry pushed off from the tree and faced his friend. "I will tell him — not yet, but soon." After he had completed his list by calling on Miss Bellamy tomorrow. "Now, explain to me how you came to be here."

Edwards shook his head and chuckled for a moment longer before he began his explanation starting with Constance's plea during the dance and ending with his strolling the garden looking for a lady in a blue dress with blonde hair and a turban that was adorned with a large sparkly bobble of some sort.

Henry scowled. "You are telling me that my sister was planning to help begin a scandal, so that I would not be able to find a respectable wife?" He knew his sister was unhappy about his change in behavior, but to keep him from finding the happiness he sought? How could she do such a thing?

"So it seems," Edwards replied. "And your Miss Linton believes you capable of being..." his voice trailed off as he studied his friend. He shook his head. "She believes you to be capable of being exactly what you have become." He shook his head again. "Respectable. I admit I had not thought it entirely possible, but here you stand, indignant at a plan for a good lark." He held up his hand as Henry opened his mouth to protest. "A year ago, we would have had a good laugh over such an escapade. Now, you look as if you are about to set off on a quest to tear a beast apart with your bare hands." He shook his head again. "Respectable," he muttered in disbelief as he pushed off the tree. "I have warned you as I said I would. You will let Miss Linton and her friend know I kept my word, will you not?"

"I will," Henry replied.

"And it would be best if you did not remain in the garden where that lady in blue might find you after I am gone. Miss Linton would be greatly displeased if that were to happen." And if Miss Linton was displeased, Miss Barrett would also be displeased. They seemed the inseparable sort. He stopped and turned toward Henry. "Perhaps you should walk with me. Then, I can heroically throw myself on any lady who attempts to accost you."

Henry rolled his eyes. However, deciding it was a wise idea not to be left alone in a place where a compromise could be staged, he joined his friend. Much to Henry's surprise, Edwards did not head directly back to the house as expected. Instead, he led Henry on a circuit of one of the paths and spoke of trivial matters.

"Crawford, Edwards."

The two gentlemen stopped walking and turned toward the path that connected to the one on which they were strolling.

"Linton," Edwards replied. "Ladies," he added with a bow.

"You are walking alone?" Linton asked Edwards with a raised brow. "With Crawford?"

Edwards made a sweeping motion. "As you can see." Then he shrugged. "I grew weary of the ballroom and wished for a respite. On my circuit, I discovered Crawford with much the same wish."

"Then, you were not walking with any lady?" Constance grimaced slightly as her brother said her name in a scolding tone. "Forgive me, but I just thought you might be strolling with a lady."

Edwards smiled. The chit was indeed intelligent as she had said. Speaking of their agreement in front of her brother in such a fashion that her brother had no clue. He shook his head. "Sadly, I have not encountered a single lady on my circuit until I met you and Miss Barrett just now."

"Not a one?" Constance asked.

"Not a one," Edwards repeated.

"And did you meet any ladies on your walk, Mr. Crawford?"

Constance sent her friend a grateful smile. She had wanted to ask that very thing but dared not.

"No, not even my sister. And I know how she likes to steal away to a garden once the ballroom gets warm." He shifted his gaze from Miss Barrett to Constance. Her pleased smile made his heart skitter. "I have nearly completed my list."

"Ah, the list," Linton said. "It was an excellent list. But then, Constance is incapable of producing shoddy work." He beamed proudly at his sister.

"Have you had any success?" he asked, turning to Henry. "Come, we will walk with you."

Henry wished that Constance was not already walking arm in arm with her friend, so that she could have been at his side. It had been so long since he had seen her or spoken to her. How he wished for everyone — especially, her brother — to disappear and leave him alone with her for a few moments. He did not want to tell her brother about his success or lack thereof. He wished only to tell her. However, that was not likely to happen. "I have learned much. However, I have not found what I am looking for on the list."

"You have not?"

Henry tipped his head. Was there a hopeful tone to Constance's voice? Or was he merely hearing what he wished to hear? "I am afraid I have not."

"That is unfortunate," Linton said.

Henry shook his head. "No, it is not, for it has helped me know precisely what I wish for in a wife."

"Do you have someone in mind?" Edwards asked, intently studying the nearly non-existent stars in the cloudy sky and avoiding looking at Henry, who was glaring at him.

Constance glanced over her shoulder toward Henry. Had he found someone? Her heart thumped a heavy beat in her chest.

Catching her eye, he winked and smiled. "Since I have not had a chance to speak to the lady or her brother, I shall refrain from answering."

"That seems to be a confirmation," said Linton.

Henry shrugged. "Perhaps it is."

Constance's brows furrowed.

Henry glanced at his companions and then certain that neither would notice, silently formed the word "you."

Her? He wished to marry her? Constance's eyes grew wide, and her mouth dropped open for a moment, then slid into a pleased smile before she turned back around. She squeezed Evelyn's arm. Oh, this was very good news. He loved her and not another.

"When do you plan to speak to the lady?" Edwards was smirking as he continued his appraisal of the night sky.

"I must complete my list first," Henry replied. "So, the day after tomorrow."

"Well, I shall wish you happy now, my friend," Edwards said as they approached the house. "Better you than I," he bowed and then, taking his leave of the group, slipped through the terrace door ahead of them.

Chapter 10

For the first morning in two weeks, Constance entered the breakfast room ready to eat a healthy dose of food. Her stomach rumbled in anticipation as she slathered a piece of fresh brown bread with sweet cream. She took a bite and savoured the flavour as she poured a cup of tea. She lifted the cup and drew a deep breath, sucking in the aroma of the tea. She felt rested and hungry and perfect.

One more day and Henry would return to her. She smiled and took a sip of her tea. He loved her. He had said so last night in the garden. She no longer needed to worry about him falling for a lady she had set in his path.

She lifted her cheek to receive a kiss from her brother as he entered.

He placed his paper next to his plate. "You are looking well this morning."

"I am feeling well," Constance replied. "It was a lovely ball, was it not?"

Linton's brows furrowed as he took a slow sip of his tea. "You do not like balls."

"True, on most occasions I do not, but last night's was rather wonderful. The way the decor twinkled in the candlelight was rather remarkable. I would imagine Mrs. Belmont had the servants polishing things for weeks before hand."

Her brother took another slow sip of his tea as he studied her. "The decor was remarkable?"

She nodded and, taking a large bite of her bread, sighed with pleasure.

"Are you well?"

"Is Constance ill?" Aunt Gwladys asked as she entered.

"She was just telling me how the decor at the ball last night was remarkable."

There was no little amount of disbelief in her brother's tone and for good reason. Constance rarely commented on such things.

"It is about time she started to notice these things," said his aunt, a pleased smile spreading across her face. "Perhaps a gentleman has finally caught her eye. Things like that often awaken a lady's appreciation of homely things. Yes," she said as she poured her cup of tea, "a touch of love often sets a lady to imagining how she will present her own home for such affairs as balls."

"A gentleman?" Linton's eyes were wide and shifting from his aunt to his sister and back. "What gentleman?"

"Was it Mr. Delaney, dear?" Aunt Gwladys asked.

"Oh, no, he was dreadful," said Constance. "Such a bore and not very enlightened."

Aunt Gwladys scowled. "You barely spoke to any of the other gentlemen who partnered you."

"I barely spoke to Mr. Delaney. He, on the other hand, could not stop speaking about everything that pleased him and why his was the only real opinion that mattered. Mine was of no value whatsoever."

"Truly?" her aunt asked in surprise. "He always struck me as a more modest sort of fellow."

"He most certainly is not modest," Constance said firmly.

"Then what made the ball so delightful?" asked her brother as he opened his paper.

Constance shrugged. "I do not know. It just was." Her cheeks warmed at the lie. She knew precisely what — or who — had made the evening delightful. However, she could not tell her brother that.

Her brother scrutinized her for a moment longer before harrumphing and turning to enjoy his paper as he ate. His eyes ran over each headline just as they always did. It was his way. He would scan the various items and then select those that interested him the most to read first before continuing to the others.

"Does it have an account of the ball? It was quite a crush," Aunt Gwladys said over her eggs. "Mrs. Belmont would be delighted to have made the papers, and Constance is correct in saying it was a lovely affair."

"Well," Linton looked up at his aunt and smiled, "There will be rejoicing at the Belmonts today." He folded the paper so he could read the account aloud.

The event of the season seems to have been held last night at the Belmonts' home. The ballroom glittered and was filled to overflowing with eager young ladies and dashing gentlemen. Though the music was without compare, the activities were not confined to dancing. A sumptuous supper was served, and many found or lost their fortunes in the card room.

Of course, as with any soiree worthy of note, there were those activities which were not sanctioned by the hostess but are, perhaps, more tantalizing in their relation to our readers. For instance, Mr. F has once again found himself with empty pockets, and it is said that his coffers are quickly depleting. It is the advice of this writer that he soon finds himself a wealthy wife and perhaps one that is better at cards than he is should he wish to try to recover the sums he has lost of late.

Speaking of those who seem to have not learned from past mistakes, Mr. C, after a few weeks of playing the part of a proper gent, was once again said to be keeping cozy company with Lady S.J. in the garden. Hopefully, Lord S.J. will be more forgiving of such an indiscretion than Mr. R was.

Constance snapped her mouth shut as her brother finished reading. "Read that last part again." Her heart raced. It could not say what she thought it said. Henry had not been in the garden with anyone.

Her brother grimaced and shook his head. "You did your best."

"But it is not true!" Tears welled up in her eyes. "He was alone in the garden. You saw him. You heard him. He was alone." She wiped a tear from her cheek.

"He said he was alone," her brother agreed, "but that does not mean he was alone."

"Yes, it does!" She glared at her brother through her tears. "Do you think him a liar?"

"It is not that," Linton began.

"Do you think him a liar?" Constance repeated.

"No, but would he have shared such behaviour in front of ladies? His answer might have been different if he were just speaking to me."

Constance shook her head. "No, you are wrong. That paper is wrong." She stood and paced back and forth next to the table.

"Connie," her brother's tone begged her to be reasonable.

"No. Mr. Edwards warned him just as he promised. That story is a lie, not Henry."

Her brother's left brow rose. "Explain."

"And I do hope your explanation includes why a Miss

L was seen entering an alcove with Mr. E," Aunt Gwladys stood beside Linton's chair. She had come to see the account of the ball with her own eyes. "Your brother stopped reading before he got to that part."

Linton snatched the paper away from his aunt and groaned as he read it.

Constance's eyes grew wide. "Did it only mention Miss L, not Miss B?"

"Evelyn was with you?" her aunt asked in astonishment.

"You are ruined," Linton held his head in his hands. "This is what I get for allowing you to help someone like Crawford." He shuddered and then pushed to his feet.

"I can explain," said Constance, grabbing her brother's arm. "It is not as it seems."

Linton tugged his arm away from her. "You can fill in any missing details when I return with your intended."

"With my what?" Constance's hand flew to her throat. No, he was not saying what she thought. He was not going to force her to marry Mr. Edwards.

"You are ruined," he repeated. "Everyone knows Edwards is a rake, and any lady meeting with him in an alcove will be presumed to be — " he waved his hand instead of saying the words. "You are ruined," he said for a third time, his jaw set in a firm line. "There is no other option."

"I will not marry him," Constance whispered as she sank into a chair. "I cannot."

"We will discuss that when I return."

Constance exhaled as if someone had punched her in the stomach. Her hand covered her mouth, and she closed her eyes as her brother left the room. She could not marry Mr. Edwards. She loved Henry, and he loved her. He had said so. A sob tore through her body, and her stomach lurched.

"Come, my dear," her aunt said, placing an arm around her shoulder. "Let's get you to your room where you can lie down and explain to me what all this nonsense is about."

~*~*~

Henry descended the steps of his house two at a time. After one last call today, his list would be completed, and he could return to Linton's and beg him for permission to court and eventually marry Constance.

He whistled a jolly tune as he mounted his horse and made his way toward the park. A bit of fresh air, a good breakfast, and then one call. He pulled in a deep breath. His happiness was very close; he could almost feel it now. Constance had smiled at his admission of wanting to marry her. His chances were very good if he could get her brother to agree with him.

"Crawford!"

Henry turned toward the barouche that was coming toward him. "St. James," he greeted with a tip of his hat.

The rather portly gentleman waved Henry over.

"How can I be of service, my lord?"

"You can learn to be discreet," the man answered, scooting to the side of the carriage closest to Henry. "I do not care what you do with my wife so long as it does not cost me money or the embarrassment of having her name or mine in the paper. I find life at home is much more pleasant when she is kept happy with whatever hobby she might find to delight herself."

"I beg your pardon? I do not understand your meaning."

Lord St. James chortled. "Very well, we shall pretend the bit in the paper did not exist. Just do try to be discreet next time." He started to move back to the center of his bench.

"What bit in the paper?" Henry's sense of confusion was turning to one of dread.

"The Belmont's garden," Lord St. James whispered.

"I did not see your wife in the garden last night if that is what you are saying. In fact, I was not even aware she was at the ball."

"That is not how the paper tells it."

The dread Henry had felt earlier was growing into panic. "What does the paper say?"

"Only that you were seen in the garden together last night, and then it suggests I might be displeased much like Rushworth was. However, I am not. As long as she continues to fulfill her duties to me, I do not care what else she might get up to with you."

"What was she wearing last night?" Things were beginning to come together in Henry's mind. His sister was a good friend of Lady St. James, who was blonde.

"Some blue concoction that cost me far more than it was worth," grumbled Lord St. James. His lips pursed and his brows drew together. "You truly did not see her last night?"

Henry shook his head. "Not that the truth matters now, does it?"

Lord St. James tugged at the buttons which were doing a valiant job of keeping his gaping jacket closed over his round belly. "No, I suppose it doesn't. However, no harm done."

"No harm done?" Henry nearly shouted. "I am to call on a lady I would actually like to have accept my offer of marriage, and neither she nor her brother are as understanding as you, my lord."

The man shrugged. "I do not write the papers, but that does put you in a difficult position, now doesn't it?"

Henry nodded and bit the tip of the glove on his thumb as he thought for a moment. There had to be a way around this. "Have you checked the veracity of the statement with your wife?"

The gentleman in the barouche blinked. "Why should I do that?"

Henry shrugged. "I don't know." He shook his head and sighed. "I thank you for your understanding, my lord, but I assure you that I have no desire to bed your wife and most certainly did not have a rendezvous with her in the Belmonts' garden." He tipped his hat to the gentleman once again and blew out a breath. Where should he go? How might he fix this? He needed Linton to accept him. Perhaps he would come upon an idea while he rode.

~*~*~

Henry lifted the knocker and let it fall for a second time on the door of a fine Mayfair home. He turned his hat in his hand and counted. When he reached twenty if the door had not opened he would knock again. He had decided on his way to the park that he must start his day by completing his list. Miss Bellamy deserved a call, and though he knew he was likely not to gain entrance to see her, he was determined to at least call on her mother.

He was just about to lift the knocker a third time when the door opened.

"It is early, sir." The Bellamy's butler looked down his nose at Henry.

"I do apologize, but it is rather important that I see Mrs. Bellamy." Henry was certain he saw a look of confusion pass over the features of the staid servant. "I am afraid my cards are at home, but if you would tell her that Mr. Crawford would greatly appreciate three minutes of her time. I will even speak to her in the foyer. I do not need to be shown to a drawing room."

The butler motioned for him to enter.

"Tell her I will not leave until she has seen me," Henry

added once he was inside the house. "I will wait here." He took a seat on a chair next to a narrow table that stood in front of a large mirror and watched the butler amble down the hall to what Henry assumed was the breakfast room. Where else would a lady be at this hour of the day if she were not still in her room dressing?

He tapped his toe as he waited and ran the brim of his hat back and forth through his fingers. Thankfully, it was only a few minutes until the lady of the house appeared.

Henry rose to greet her. "I do apologize Mrs. Bellamy, but as I was on my way to take my ride this morning a bit of news was brought to my attention. It seems my name was seen in the paper by Lord St. James."

She was still scowling at him, but her eyebrows had risen in interest. It was likely she would hear him out rather than shooing him on his way as he expected her to do.

"Someone was seen in the garden with his wife last night, but I assure you it was not me. However, I understand that you will not want me to call on your daughter any longer, which is just as well since I do not think we would suit. She is a lovely lady, and some gentleman will be happy to secure her hand, but that gentleman is not me." He bowed. "Thank you for your time. I will leave you to your day."

"It was not you?" Mrs. Bellamy questioned.

He shook his head. "It was not me."

She shook her head. "I am not certain I believe you."

"I understand. That is only natural."

"Thank you for calling," Mrs. Bellamy said, motioning to the door and beginning to walk that direction. "You know I only gave you a chance because you were with Mr. Linton," she commented as they moved the few steps to the entrance, "and he and his sister have always been so proper. However, it seems I was wrong. Perhaps not in you, if you are telling the truth, but in Miss Linton."

The butler had opened the door, and Henry was about to step through it but her words stopped him. "I beg your pardon?"

"Have you not seen the paper?" Mrs. Bellamy asked.

"No, I read it after I ride. As I said, Lord St. James informed me that my name had been mentioned alongside his wife's. Did the paper mention Miss Linton?"

"Oh, yes. It seems she was seen in an alcove with a rake."

There was a disturbing look of amusement in the lady's eyes. What was it about some women that made them delight in the downfall of another?

"You are certain it was Miss Linton?"

"Oh, no names were given, of course, but I am nearly certain it was her," replied Mrs. Bellamy.

Henry thanked her once more for her time and stepped out onto the Bellamy's front step. The paper. He needed to read that blasted paper before he did anything else. However, if it was true that Miss Linton's name had been linked to Edwards, Edwards was about to find himself betrothed to the lady Henry loved, and there was no way, Henry was going to allow that to happen.

Chapter 11

"Pardon me," Henry excused himself as he brushed past a lady standing behind what appeared to be her daughter, who was admiring a fan the shop assistant was displaying. It was a pretty fan — blue with golden embellishments, quite like his sister would fancy. She did love exquisite accessories. However, fans were not what Henry had come to Pall Mall to find. He was in search of that particular collector of fans and clothing and all that was contained within the walls of this establishment.

After having an abbreviated breakfast while reading the paper he still clutched in his hand, he had gone to call on Dr. and Mrs. Grant in hopes of finding his sister and learning exactly how the account bearing his name ended up in the paper. She was not at home, however, so after spending an appropriate amount of time so as not to be thought too rudely abrupt in his visit, he had come here — a store he knew his sister often frequented.

He was not wrong, for at the counter just beyond the

third partition in the store, stood his sister, wafting the fragrances of various boxes and bottles.

"There is none there that will hide the pungent stench of a talebearer or the acrid aroma of a liar," he hissed near her ear, causing her to jump.

"Henry!" she chided. "You should know better than to creep up on a lady." She held the bottle out to him. "What do you think of this fragrance?" She swept her hand across the top of the opening sending a whiff of perfume towards him.

He had not meant to answer her question. He was here to speak with her about serious matters, not help her choose a scent. However, the faint bouquet hinting strongly of roses caused his lips to curl upward with pleasure. "I like it very much," he said.

"I thought you might," his sister replied with a sly smile. "A certain young debutante wears this very one."

"Yes," he said, his eyes narrowing, "she does."

"Are you here to purchase a bottle for Miss Linton?" Mary's eyes twinkled with amusement.

"I am here to speak with you," he said, placing the rather worse-for-the-wear paper on the counter. Then he turned and leaned in front of her. "Your help will not be needed for a few moments," he said over his shoulder to the shop assistant. "Are you here alone?"

Mary crossed her arms and tapped her foot. "No, Sarah is with me."

Good. She was annoyed. He looked down the counter on which he was leaning and then around his sister to the counter on the opposite side of the store. There, trying on a necklace, was Lady Sarah St. James.

"Then I am in luck," he replied. "I am certain one of you can tell me how this false account ended up in the paper."

"A false account?" Mary's brows drew together, but her eyes held no true perplexity.

"This one," he said, lifting the paper and after clearing his throat loudly enough to draw some attention, began reading.

> "*Speaking of those who seem to have not learned from past mistakes, Mr. C,* —

"That is me," he explained to an eager listener on his right.

> — *after a few weeks of playing the part of proper gent,* —

"I have been conducting myself very well, have I not?" he asked his sister.

> — *was once again said to be keeping cozy company with Lady S.J.* —

"That is you, Lady St. James," he called across the aisle, holding up the paper and pointing to the article as she turned to look his direction before he continued reading.

> — *in the garden. Hopefully, Lord S.J. will be more forgiving of such an indiscretion than Mr. R was.*"

"He was right gracious when I met him on my way to the park this morning. You'll not have a worry there, my lady," he called once again across the aisle. "I say, it came as a shock to me, however, as I did not even know you attended the Belmonts' soiree."

He placed the paper back on the counter. "It is all there," he said to the lady who was peering over his hand to see what he had been reading. "How it got there is what I would like to know." He crossed his arms and glared at his sister.

"Oh, who knows how any of these things end up in the paper. Imaginations are so full of fancy," said Lady St. James, who had crossed the aisle to stand next to Mary.

"I happen to believe that there was someone who fanned the flames of this reporter's imagination," he said, not allowing his glower to waver from his sister.

Lady St. James's laugh was light and nervous. "I am sure we could not tell you if such a thing happened."

Henry shook his head. "No, you could tell me. You just will not tell me, but, I assure you that you could. For you see, I have had some time to ponder how this flagrant falsehood came to appear in a report of the Belmonts' ball, and it occurred to me that one might plan a scandal to damage another's reputation. However, due to one thing or another, that scandal might not come to pass as one cannot always control all the principal players. For instance, a gentleman, whom you plan to seduce, might not be in the garden as expected." He raised an eyebrow and gave Lady St. James a pointed look. "That would ruin one's plan, would it not? And, I imagine, if one's plan is thwarted, one might find that highly disagreeable and resort to other means. Such as, shall we say, concocting a story to be printed in the paper. That should achieve the initially desired outcome — the ruination of my burgeoning respectable reputation." He stared hard at Lady St. James. "I know what you had planned." It was rather gratifying to see her eyes widen just a bit at the comment.

"Henry," Mary began, only to be cut off by her brother.

"Mr. Crawford," Henry corrected with a slight growl. "You may refer to me as Mr. Crawford."

Her mouth dropped open. "But you are my brother," she protested.

"And you are my sister," he ground out, "yet, you would scheme to see me disgraced. Where is your heart? At this moment, I would very much doubt you possess such an organ if I had not seen it over the years as we grew up." He shook his head. "When you find your heart, then you may call me Henry again. I cannot erase the connection we have through parents, though presently I would very much wish to do so."

"Mr. Crawford," cooed Lady St. James. "It is but a bit of gossip. Surely one does not sever ties over a tawdry story. Another will appear, and this will be forgotten."

He shook his head. "No. It is not just a piece of lint to be flicked away, as this has perhaps ruined my final chance at happiness. You see, I had decided to make an offer to a lady of the best character. However, she, just like Miss Price, the last time my sister meddled in my affairs, will likely not accept me if she thinks I continue down the path of the libertine — and rightly so!"

"This fit of pique is over that little Linton girl?" scoffed Lady St. James. "My dear Mr. Crawford, she will soon come to know that these things are just the way of the world. Marriage might begin with the promise of constancy, but then, well, boredom sets in and one must find his or her entertainments elsewhere. Oh, I know a gentleman must secure his estate, but he need not hide himself away at it."

Henry looked at her in disgust.

Lady St. James lifted the paper from the counter. "And it seems the estimable Miss Linton is not as virtuous as you claim."

"That," Henry said, snatching the paper from Lady St. James, "is also a falsehood. I know precisely why Miss Linton met with Mr. Edwards last night." He tipped his head at his sister's smirk. "As I suspect, so do you." The flick of Lady St. James' brow and a minuscule shrug gave him to know he was correct.

"Henry, do you really wish to be so dull?" asked Mary, laying a hand on his arm.

"Mr. Crawford," he corrected, lifting her hand off his arm and letting it drop. "I suppose what I wish to be would be considered dull by your lot. You who seek husbands to buy you bobbles and gowns and who will expect no more in return than to warm his bed long enough to produce the requisite heir and a spare — oh, and to be discreet. Having his name bandied about in the paper is not pleasing, you see."

He shook his head. "What sort of husband does not care for his wife beyond that? What husband worth anything allows his wife to run off with the likes of me and does not chase her down and beg her to return? You may ask Mr. Rushworth that question. Perhaps his answer will be better than mine. For I would say, it is a cold husband who behaves so."

He chuckled, a low and bitter sound. "I will not be such a man. If I cannot marry a lady I love in such a way, I will not marry."

The bitterness he felt at the view of marriage Lady St. James had presented crept into the smile he turned on her. His uncle had held the same views, and though his uncle always seemed to be enjoying himself, he never seemed satisfied. There was always the need for another flirtation, for another conquest, for another mistress.

"If you will excuse me, I must go call on Linton before he has signed over his sister to what is left of my reprobate friend."

He bowed, but then before he left, tapped on the counter. "That fragrance, the one my sister was last admiring," he said to the store assistant, "will you hold one of those for me until tomorrow?"

The man's eyes grew wide in surprise, but he assured Henry that he would.

"Very good," Henry said with a nod. "I will return, and if I am successful, purchase that bottle for the future Mrs. Crawford." A smile spread across his face and a faint feeling akin to hope crept into his heart at the appellation. Surely, Linton would allow him to marry Constance in Edwards's place.

"Wait a moment," called a lady from the crowd that had gathered during Henry's reading of the paper. "You mean to tell us that this story about you is not true?"

Henry nodded. "Did we have a rendezvous in the garden last night, Lady St. James?"

Her jaw clenched, and her chin lifted. "No," she admitted.

"And Miss Linton?" the lady asked.

"She heard Lady St. James planning to create the scenario described in the paper, and not wishing to see me fall victim to such scheming, she enlisted the help of my friend, Mr. Edwards, to warn me. She is, as she always has been, without fault and far too good for me."

"But you love her?" There was a tone of wistfulness to the lady's question.

"With all that I am," Henry answered. "I only hope I can

prove myself worthy of her and gain her brother's approval of my suit."

The lady sighed. "I wish you well."

"As do I," said a familiar voice. "Might I join you on your call, Mr. Crawford? I think my account of what I have witnessed here will go a long way in swaying Trefor Linton's opinion. His aunt and I are dear friends, after all."

Henry bowed and extended his arm. "I would be delighted to have your company."

Mrs. Barrett placed her hand on his arm, and together, they left the store.

Chapter 12

Being on horse and not in a carriage, Henry arrived at the Linton townhouse before Mrs. Barrett. He paced the walk in front of the door for a few minutes, attempting to wait patiently for the lady to join him. He would be less likely to be refused admittance if he were accompanied by Mrs. Kendrick's particular friend. He was certain he could just see the Barrett carriage when the door to the house opened behind him.

"It is about time you arrived," Mrs. Kendrick said, pulling her wrap tightly around her shoulders and descending to the street to greet him. "You have come to marry Constance, have you not?" Her eyes held no amusement. They were as serious as he had ever seen them.

"I had thought to, yes," Henry replied slowly.

Aunt Gwladys blew out a breath in relief. "Thank the Good Lord in heaven above. Now, before my niece expires in a fit of vapours." She turned and hurried toward the house.

Henry took one last look down the street. He was positive that carriage belonged to Mrs. Barrett. He should wait and see her safely inside.

"Are you coming?" Mrs. Kendrick called.

"Mrs. Barrett was to join me," said Henry, pointing to the carriage that was nearly at its destination.

Mrs. Kendrick looked from the carriage back to Henry. "Very well, I suppose it is only proper for you to wait for her, but please do not be long. Trefor is anxious to receive your confirmation of Mr. Edwards's account about his purpose in finding you in the garden."

Henry assured her that he would indeed hurry, and he did. Mrs. Barrett seemed to understand the urgency of how things likely stood and was herself unwilling to be sedate in manners.

"Allow me to enter ahead of you," she whispered to Henry as they approached the door to the sitting room. "Mr. Linton will be forced to act appropriately to greet a lady, and that should save you any undue censure."

Henry did as instructed and followed closely behind Mrs. Barrett when she entered the room. Linton, as expected, straightened his coat, bowed, and said all the proper things — in a rather strained tone, but he said them.

"Crawford." Linton's tone was surprisingly flat and not the growl Henry had expected.

"Linton," Henry acknowledged, though his eyes did not move from the sight that had arrested him when he entered the room.

Edwards sat in a chair, his head tipped back, a cloth held to his nose while Constance held a compress to his eye. It was not as if he did not expect to see Edwards with a few injuries. Linton had promised more than that if either of them should ever compromise his sister. Apparently, even a compromise by chance was not to go unanswered.

However, more concerning to Henry was the redness of Constance's eyes and nose. She had obviously been crying, and not just a few tears. Her face was drawn, and her expression tight as if struggling to compose herself enough to stay upright. The hand not holding the compress to Edwards's head was gripping the chair so tightly that her knuckles were white. And if he was not mistaken, he had seen a small tremor pass through her body when she saw him enter.

"Allow me," Henry said, crossing the room. "You should sit down. I can hold that cloth." He placed his hand over hers on Edwards's head and slipped an arm around her waist since he could see her trembling beside him.

"A chair for you sister, Linton," he snapped. "What have you done to her?"

"Me?" It was not a growl, but more of a roar and much more like what Henry had expected from Linton.

"Yes, you," Henry lifted the compress off his friend's head. There was no blood. He lay the cloth back down.

"If you hold still, this will stay here," he said to Edwards.

"Come," he said softly to Constance, "you must sit." Henry led her over to a settee and sat down beside her.

"It was not me whose name was in the paper," Linton sputtered. "I was not the one sneaking into alcoves or meeting with married women in gardens."

"Neither was Mr. Crawford," Mrs. Barrett interjected. "Mr. Edwards was likely sneaking into alcoves, but not for any nefarious reasons where your sister or my daughter are concerned." She had taken Henry's place at Edwards's side and lifted the compress from off his eye. "However, I shall thank you not to be in any dark corner with my daughter in the future."

Edwards nodded and mumbled his agreement.

"Good," she replaced the covering over his eye. "Evelyn had wanted to call on you as soon as she saw the paper, Miss Linton, but I told her it would be best to let things settle a mite and call tomorrow. She agreed but was so distraught over the whole ordeal that I could not persuade her to accompany me on my shopping trip."

Constance attempted to smile at her friend's mother. She knew how dearly Evelyn loved to shop.

"I nearly stayed home myself," Mrs. Barrett took a seat next to Mrs. Kendrick. "But I am very glad I did not, for it was a very enlightening experience, " she said with a smile.

Linton cleared his throat. "Might we discuss shopping later?" he asked.

"Oh, certainly," she agreed, "but I do think my tale

would help wrap matters up here," she motioned to Mr. Edwards and then to Constance and Henry, "with all due haste."

"Do be seated, Trefor," commanded his aunt.

Linton did as instructed. "Very well, Mrs. Barrett, if you think your story will help me, I will listen."

"I was intent on purchasing a fan for Evelyn's birthday and was making my selection when Mr. Crawford entered looking for all the world as if the devil were at his heels." She chuckled. "The devil was not at his heels but rather admiring a necklace."

She leaned toward Mrs. Kendrick and whispered loudly. "Lady St. James." She turned to address the room again. "And she was not alone. Miss Crawford was with her."

Linton's eyes turned from Mrs. Barrett to Henry.

"There was a scheme in which my sister played a part," he began.

"To see you compromised and considered unfit as a candidate for many young ladies?" Linton asked.

Henry nodded. "But it came to naught because Edwards warned me of it."

"And Edwards knew of it because of Connie."

"Yes," Henry confirmed, "that is what he told me when he found me in the garden. I am uncertain how my sister found out that it was your sister and Edwards who warned me, but judging from her reactions this morning, she knew." He took Constance's hand. "I cannot express how grieved I am that she has caused you harm."

"It was not your doing," Constance whispered.

"So, Edwards was telling me the truth," Linton stated.

"Yes, Edwards was telling the truth," Edwards said from behind the cloth he still held to his nose.

"The fact still remains that all of London knows you were in an alcove with my sister," Linton growled. "And you know what they will think that was about."

"Oh, not any longer," said Mrs. Barrett.

"I beg your pardon?" Linton said, turning towards the lady.

"Mr. Crawford did a valiant job of defending not only his honour but that of your sister as well."

Henry could tell from the glint in the woman's eye that she was enjoying revealing small portions of the events of the morning while keeping others concealed.

Linton crossed his arms. "Please continue."

"It was staged almost as well as any play could be with Mr. Crawford leaning against the perfumery counter in front of his sister and reading that dreadful article in the paper loudly enough for everyone to hear, and then declaring his wish to be rid of his sister for her behaviour." Her hand flew dramatically to her heart. "And then to declare that any man who allows his wife to run off with another without chasing after her was," she looked at Henry, "what was the word you used?"

The right side of Henry's mouth tipped up – as if she could not remember! "Cold," he answered. "Not a husband at all, really. Certainly, not the sort I intend to be."

"And then he said if he could not marry for love, he would not marry at all!"

She leaned toward Mrs. Kendrick. "If he did not already have a particular lady in mind and had he not announced it to the gathered throng, I am certain there would have been more than one mother pushing her daughter in his path as he exited. However, as it stood, having declared his intentions to attempt to secure this particular young lady, who he assured them was without reproach, they merely let him pass. And the tale of how Lady St. James attempted to compromise Mr. Crawford and the gallant part Miss Linton and Mr. Edwards played in thwarting the scheme will be well circulated by tomorrow. Indeed, I dare say it shall be in the paper. I certainly have not witnessed such a display — it truly was newsworthy."

"Am I to assume, Crawford," Linton began, "that all of London knows the name of this particular lady whom you wish to take for a wife?"

Henry swallowed. This was not perhaps how he had intended to broach the subject with Linton, but it was probably no less comfortable than if he had found himself in Linton's office attempting to plead his case. At least here, it seemed he had Mrs. Barrett to come to his aid should he need it. He nodded. "Yes."

"I told you he would marry her," said Edwards, who now held a compress only to his eye as his nose had stopped bleeding, "but you were so bent on dragging me from my house, that you would not listen."

Henry scowled at Edwards. "You promised not to say anything about that."

Edwards let out a short burst of laughter. "When Linton has you by the neck, you say what you have to say to retain your life."

"So, you wish to marry my sister?" Linton's arms were still folded, and his expression had not softened in the least.

"Yes, if you will allow it, and she will have me." Henry kept his eyes fixed on Linton even though he wished to see what Constance's reaction was to his declaration. He rubbed his hands nervously on his knees until a small hand captured one of them, and he felt as if he could once again breathe. "I love her."

Linton's eyes narrowed. "I believe I warned both of you that such a thing could happen when you began this agreement to help you improve."

"You did," Henry agreed. "You also told me you would kill me if I broke her heart."

"I did, and that promise still holds true. Do not break her heart. Treat her well, Crawford." A smile spread across his face. "Not that she will ever allow you to treat her otherwise."

Constance gasped. "I have not yet said I will accept him." She would, of course, but it was rather bothersome that her brother would just give her away without consulting her.

Linton chuckled and stood. "I am not so thick headed as you might think, my dear sister. If you will remember, I asked you two weeks ago if you would accept him, and you said you would. I could tell how little you wished to give him that list." He winked at her and then turned to the rest of the room. "Now, if you would care to join me in the breakfast room for a celebratory cup of tea, we can let Crawford get on with making his offer, so it can be accepted."

"I have your permission?" Henry asked.

Linton nodded. "You have proven yourself worthy, first by learning all the things Connie taught you, then by doing as I asked and staying away from her for two weeks, and finally, by choosing her above your own sister. Those are not the actions of a man who will waver or neglect his responsibilities." He clapped Henry on the shoulder and then bent to kiss his sister's forehead before leaving the room and closing the door firmly behind him.

Henry sat for a moment, staring at the door. Linton approved of him. Linton — all that was proper, never-waver-from-the-straight-and-narrow Linton — was trusting him, Henry Crawford, with the precious heart of his sister. The idea was not displeasing. It was actually quite the opposite, but it was a little unsettling.

"A proper gentleman," Constance began, "does not sit mutely by when he intends to make an offer of marriage to a lady."

Henry smiled at the familiar tone of instruction she used. "Are you well?" he asked, laying a hand on her cheek, which had grown rosy.

She nodded. "I am now."

"I am so very sorry that you have had to endure all this." He removed his hand from her cheek and took her hands in his. "I called on Miss Bellamy this morning after Lord St. James made me aware of the article in the paper — or, more accurately, I called on Miss Bellamy's mother and told her that I did not think her daughter and I would suit. My list is complete."

Constance shook her head. "You called on Mrs. Bellamy even with such a scandal in the paper?"

He nodded. "I made a promise to a very dear lady whom I love with all my heart that I would complete that list, and I will never, ever, in a thousand years, break a promise that I have made to her."

Constance blinked at the happy tears that gathered in her eyes.

"I love you, Constance Linton. Not as I loved before." He shook his head. "Until now, I only sought to win the heart and admiration of another, and while I still long to have your heart, I no longer wish to retain mine. It is yours. I lay it at your feet and ask that you will care for it from this day until death parts us with its eternal sleep. Will you accept both it and me? Will you be my wife?" He lifted her hands and softly kissed her knuckles as he looked into her eyes.

A smile split Constance's face. "Yes. Yes." Her head bobbed up and down. "I will gladly be your wife."

She pulled her hands from his grasp and threw her arms around his neck. "Oh, how I love you!"

He chuckled as he stood and pulled her into his embrace. "I did not think a proper chit threw herself at a gentleman." He squeezed her tightly and ran a hand in a soothing motion up and down her back.

Constance laughed against his chest and attempted to pull away.

"I am not complaining," he said quickly. "I am only unsure what a proper gentleman does when such a thing happens. I know what my former self would do." He tipped her chin up, so he could look into her eyes. "My former self would kiss you."

Indeed, his every fiber shouted at him to do that very thing, but he would not presume. He would wait for her permission. That, he thought to himself, was likely what a proper gentleman would do.

"As long as the lady in your arms is your wife, or will be, and you are in private as we are now, I think a kiss would be just the thing." She could feel her cheeks growing exceedingly warm as her heart quickened its pace within her chest. How she had wanted him to kiss her since that day in the library two weeks ago!

His head moved towards hers. "I promise you that I will never kiss another — only you."

"And you will never break that promise?" She knew in her heart that he would not, but she longed to hear it from his lips.

"Never, though my life be required of me to keep it."

She sighed as his lips finally met hers in that magical last first kiss.

Henry was no novice. He had kissed many ladies. And while this kiss, just as those others, stirred his desires for the lady in his arms, no kiss had ever tasted so sweet or flooded his body with the joy that this kiss did. For with this kiss came an exchange of hearts. His was no longer his own, and hers? Well, that was a precious treasure, and he would willingly spend the rest of his days proving himself worthy of such a gift.

Before You Go

If you enjoyed this book, be sure to let others know by leaving a review.

~*~*~

Want to know when book four, *Tom: To Secure His Legacy*, will be available?

You can always know what's new with my books by subscribing to my mailing list.

(There will, of course, be a thank you gift for joining because I think my readers are awesome!)

Book News from Leenie Brown

(http://eepurl.com/bSreI1)

~*~*~

Turn the page to read an excerpt of another one of Leenie's books

Charles: To Discover His Purpose Excerpt

[*Other Pens, Mansfield Park, Episode 2* follows Charles Edwards as he attempts to scheme his way into getting a kiss from Miss Barrett.]

CHAPTER 1

Charles Edwards squinted into the late afternoon sun – it was an action that he could almost do without any discomfort. The swelling around his eye had subsided, and soon, the bruising would fade to a nasty yellow and then disappear. Until that happened, he would continue to take his rides by wandering from one street to the next rather than face the taunting and questioning looks he was guaranteed to receive in the parks.

While it was an excellent way to avoid censure from his peers, it was dashed boring trotting up and down streets without so much as a single friend with whom to converse. Had he earned his scars more gallantly, perhaps he would not feel the need to hide them. To have been injured in a boxing match or defense of some lady's honor would make his bruises more of a badge than a blemish. However, since everyone in town had likely read that blasted article in the paper, the raised eyebrows from overprotective matrons and giggles from their charges would be unbearable. And then, there would be the gentlemen. He shook his head. Had he received a blackened eye from Trefor Linton for actually doing something inappropriate with Linton's sister, Constance, his friends would just laugh and clap him on the shoulder before filling his glass with some libation at his club.

But, he had not been caught doing anything improper. In fact, it was much worse than just not being found dallying with a debutante. He had been attempting to be gallant. He would do his best not to be put in such a situation again! Honourable actions and favours to ladies who were offering none in return must be avoided for they only led to broken noses, disgrace, and lonely rambles up less well-to-do streets.

"Mr. Edwards?"

Charles drew his horse to a stop just in front of a carriage that was standing at the ready to receive a lovely young woman. He had not bothered to take note of her since this was not the part of town where the finest flowers of the season resided.

"Miss Linton," he said doffing his hat. "Is Crawford with you?" He nodded to the carriage.

"No," Constance Linton replied with a smile, "though he very much wanted to be. It is just Evelyn and me."

His brows furrowed. Evelyn? The name sounded familiar.

"Miss Barrett," Constance clarified.

"Ah, Miss Barrett. Of course. How negligent of me to not remember." How had he managed to forget her name? He certainly had not forgotten her perfectly pink lips or lithe figure. The same figure that was exiting the house to his left. She was perhaps the most enticing creature he had ever met and never sampled.

"Oh!"

Miss Barrett's lips formed such a wonderfully kissable *o*.

"Mr. Edwards," she greeted with a small curtsey. "Are you here to visit Mrs. Verity and the children?"

His brows furrowed again. "Mrs. Who?"

"Verity," Evelyn repeated. "She runs this home for children." She motioned toward the house.

"I did not know this was a home for children." His left brow rose in question. "Why are you here? None of these children are yours, I would assume."

Her eyes grew wide, and she gasped. "We are not all as reprobate as you, Mr. Edwards."

He leaned forward nonchalantly admiring her look of utter indignation. "Then, what, pray tell, are proper young ladies such as yourself and Miss Linton doing here?"

"Charitable work. You do know what that is, do you not?"

He chuckled. Miss Barret was not the sort to shy away quietly to her corner and leave him be. He liked that. "I have heard the term."

"But have you ever experienced it?" asked Constance.

He shifted his gaze to his friend, Henry Crawford's, betrothed. "No, not beyond what is expected on my father's estate."

"It's rather fulfilling," Constance replied. "Today, we taught some children their letters. It was remarkable, was it not, Evelyn?" She wore a look of sheer delight.

"And Linton approves of this?" Charles asked.

"Both he and Henry do."

Delight did not begin to describe the look in Miss Linton's eyes as she said the name Henry. One day, when he was ready to take up his mantle of responsibility, Charles hoped to find a lady who would look even half as happy saying his name as Miss Linton did at this moment.

"Trefor," Constance continued, "thought this would be a safe way to keep me occupied. My last scheme, you see, did not leave him favourably disposed to allowing me to find ways in which to make my life more interesting."

There was a mischievous gleam in both her eye and that of her friend, Evelyn. Curious, that. He had not expected anything akin to impishness from Trefor Linton's sister or any of her friends. Constance Linton was the most proper chit he had ever met, and he suspected, to be her friend, Miss Barrett must be the same.

"Is your eye feeling better?" Miss Barrett asked.

"It is, but I'll not be doing either of you any favours in the future," he replied with a smirk. "At least not unless I receive something better than a broken nose and a black eye in return."

"I can neither apologize or thank you enough," Constance replied.

She had apologized over and over and over again as she stood holding a compress to his eye in the Linton sitting room those many days ago. "I think you have said the words enough," he replied softly. "I merely jest." He would not have her feeling guilty for his injuries when it was not her doing which caused them.

Miss Barrett tipped her head as she looked up at him, a puzzled look on her face. Then, she shook herself and smiled. "We are expected at your house soon, Connie. Mother will be waiting."

"As will Trefor," she smiled, "and Henry."

Much to Charles's surprise, Miss Evelyn Barrett rolled her eyes at the tone her friend used to say Henry's name.

"Do not let me detain you, I would not wish to run afoul of any of them." He winked at Miss Barret. "At least, not until I am healed."

She gasped. "My mother has warned me about you, Mr. Edwards."

"As well she should," he replied easily. "I am dreadfully charming."

Constance had entered the carriage, but Evelyn, who remained on the street, laughed. "That is not how my mother said it." Her eyes sparkled with impertinence. Then, with a small curtsey of parting, she boarded her carriage.

Charles looked after her and tipped his hat as the door closed on those shining eyes and teasing smile. Oh, he could find great pleasure in evoking such a look from her on a regular basis. Not that he wished to spend great amounts of time with her. No, he was not the sort of gentleman to trot around behind a lady hoping for her to smile at him or laugh at his jokes. He danced; he flirted; and he stole kisses. He did not become attached. Attachments were dangerous. They led to marriage and, he fought the urge to shudder, responsibility. He was far too young for such things as that just yet.

Still, he wondered where she would be this evening and if there would be any dark corners into which she might be persuaded.

He blew out a breath. Hiding himself away from society was perhaps not the best idea in the world. It apparently was wreaking havoc on his well-ordered, carefree existence. A rogue such as himself did not stalk his prey. He simply looked for the opportunity and took it. Planning anything was far too much like being responsible. Rules, guidelines, ledgers, accounts, and all the rest that went with being a gentleman of standing belonged to his father, not Charles.

In front of him the carriage stopped, a man jumped down, the door opened, and a pretty face peered out, looking back to where he was.

He nudged his horse forward as Miss Barrett waved him towards her.

"Do you require help?" he asked as he drew near.

"No, no, we are well. Connie and I were just talking, and I thought as we were discussing how dreadful it is that you were injured on Connie's account that it would be charitable of us to offer you a place in the Linton's box at the theatre tonight."

Charles began to shake his head.

"Hear me out. Do not refuse until I have made my full request. And come forward more, I feel as if I am going to fall out of this door and onto the street."

Charles chuckled. This young woman sounded more like Linton's cantankerous Aunt Gwladys than a young lady of the ton. Most young ladies who presented themselves during the season went out of their way to appear demure to one and all – always.

"Do you scold everyone?" he teased as he did as she said.

If he had expected her to be offended, he was once again going to be surprised, for she merely smiled, batted her lashes, and replied, "No, I scold very few beyond my brother actually."

"So, I am special," he returned.

She shrugged. "Perhaps you are. Or perhaps I just find you as troublesome as Griffin."

"I think I will insist you find me special."

"Do what you will; it matters not one jot to me," she retorted.

Her words might have said she did not care, but her tone clearly said she was annoyed.

"As I was saying..."

"Before you began scolding." Charles smiled at her huff.

"Before I had to pause to give instructions."

Charles chuckled. "Continue. I shall not refuse until you have said your piece."

"Refuse? You intend to refuse?"

"Most likely. But, I have not heard your request in full, so I cannot be certain I am correct until I do. I have been wrong before."

Her brows rose, and her lips pursed for a moment as if she were holding back some retort.

"There will not be very many people in our box. If you slip in a side door or something and scurry up to the box, you will not have to have many people gawk at you."

"You think I am worried about being seen?"

"I would be if my eye were the colour of yours, and that is why you are riding here and not in a more populated place, is it not? And, I have not seen you at any events since...well..." she pointed to her eye.

"I will admit that I do not relish the whispers." Why he felt he needed to admit such a thing was beyond him. He could come up with any number of reasons to be riding where he was and for not having been at any soiree she had attended. A smile slipped slowly across his face. "Have you missed me?"

"What?" She shook her head vigorously. "No. I just noticed that I had not seen you slinking from shadow to shadow."

"If you say so."

"I do." She scowled. "Now, will you be joining us? I am certain no one would be in the least put out if you did."

"How reassuring," Charles muttered.

"Please," Constance added from the interior of the carriage. "I do feel dreadful that you have been out of society. It must be terribly boring sitting at home instead of going out."

"Who said I was sitting at home?" He smiled a lazy, suggestive smile.

"Henry," Constance replied.

Blast! Did Henry tell her everything?

"Very well, I have been hiding away. Are you happy to know my shame?"

"Only if it means you will join us," said Miss Barrett.

"Can you not muster an ounce of sympathy?" he asked

in surprise. Were not young ladies – especially those who did charity work – supposed to be compassionate?

She shook her head. "No. Not a morsel. While I am awfully sorry you were injured, I do believe you have escaped more times than you have been caught."

The lady might look like an angel, but she had a heart of ice. However, ice could be melted. In fact, it could be quite a marvelous lark to attempt to melt that ice.

"Very well, I will join you if you will but attempt to feel an ounce of pity for me."

The way her lips pursed with contained amusement was tempting.

"A full ounce?"

"Yes." He moved closer to her door. "A full ounce." He repeated the words in a low, sultry tone – slowly and deliberately. Satisfaction curled his lips as he saw her pretty nibble-worthy neck rise and fall as she swallowed.

She licked her lips. "I shall make an attempt."

"Then, I shall see you at the theatre."

"Very good."

He chuckled at the uncertainty in her voice. Again, he tipped his hat to the closed carriage door and watched it drive away before continuing on his way home to prepare for an evening of entertainment — and a play.

Acknowledgements

There are many who have had a part in the creation of this story. Some have read and commented on it. Some have proofread for grammatical errors and plot holes. Others have not even read the story and a few, I know, will never read it. However, their encouragement and belief in my ability, as well as their patience when I became cranky or when supper was late or the groceries ran low, was invaluable.

And so, I would like to say *thank you* to Zoe, Rose, Betty, Kristine, Ben, and Kyle. I feel blessed through your help, support, and understanding.

I have not listed my dear husband in the above group because, to me, he deserves his own special thank you, for without his somewhat pushy insistence that I start sharing my writing, none of my writing goals and dreams would have been met.

Other Leenie B Books

You can find all of Leenie's books at this link
or choose to explore the collections below
~*~
Other Pens, Mansfield Park
~*~
Touches of Austen Collection
~*~
Other Pens, Pride and Prejudice
~*~
Dash of Darcy and Companions Collection
~*~
Marrying Elizabeth Series
~*~
Willow Hall Romances
~*~
The Choices Series
~*~
Darcy Family Holidays
~*~
Other Novels ~ Novellas ~ Shorts

About the Author

Leenie Brown has always been a girl with an active imagination, which, while growing up, was a both an asset, providing many hours of fun as she played out stories, and a liability, when her older sister and aunt would tell her frightening tales. At one time, they had her convinced Dracula lived in the trunk at the end of the bed she slept in when visiting her grandparents!

Although it has been years since she cowered in her bed in her grandparents' basement, she still has an imagination which occasionally runs away with her, and she feeds it now as she did then — by reading!

Her heroes, when growing up, were authors, and the worlds they painted with words were (and still are) her favourite playgrounds! Now, as an adult, she spends much of her time in the regency world, playing with the characters from her favourite Jane Austen novels and those of her own creation.

When she is not traipsing down a trail in an attempt to keep up with her imagination, Leenie resides in the beautiful province of Nova Scotia with her two sons and her very own Mr. Brown (a wonderful mix of all the best of Darcy, Bingley, and Edmund with a healthy dose of the teasing Mr. Tilney and just a dash of the scolding Mr. Knightley).

Connect with Leenie Brown

E-mail:

LeenieBrownAuthor@gmail.com

Facebook:

www.facebook.com/LeenieBrownAuthor

Blog:

leeniebrown.com

Patreon:

https://www.patreon.com/LeenieBrown

Subscribe to Leenie's Mailing List:

Book News from Leenie Brown

(http://eepurl.com/bS1eI1)

Join Leenie on Austen Authors:

austenauthors.net

www.ingramcontent.com/pod-product-compliance
Lightning Source LLC
Chambersburg PA
CBHW071133200626
46817CB00018B/2934